The Invisible Woman

D L Bloom

ISBN:10:1539650316
ISBN-13:978-1539650317

DEDICATION

This book is dedicated to my beloved daughter
Nicola Jane Robinson
1971-2016

CONTENTS

ACKNOWLEDGMENT

I would like to thank Linda Sabrina and Vanessa from Page Fillers. Novel writers group Vanessa Lynne and Kate.
The writers room with Kate and all the members for support and belief. A big thank you to Claire and Jessica for help with editing, patience is a virtue.
Ian for technical support.
Last but not least to Peter for supplying me with so much material..

CHAPTER ONE

Heather was invisible. There was no doubt about it. She
stared at the dressing table mirror, there wasn't anything
or anyone looking back.. Her grey library uniform
didn't help, it just added to the grey mist before her.
Jeff gave a loud snore as he turned over and snuggled
further down into the duvet. She did what she did most
days running on automatic pilot, the alarm went off
7.30am, she showered, changed into her uniform and made
tea for herself and for her disabled mother in law Iris, who
had taken over the master bedroom of the very neat
semi-detached house. Iris had lived with her and Jeff after
she had had a stroke. Nurses came in every day but still
most of the caring was left to Heather. Jeff, although at
home all day after being made redundant thought that
men were not very good at nursing or looking after people.
He managed to make his mother a sandwich at lunchtime
and take her a cup of tea. After a hurried breakfast Heather
left at 8.15am. She just caught a flash of colour in the hall
mirror, she stopped there was a slight outline but no
defining features. Yes, her youth had long gone but now
her physical being was disappearing, she was almost but
maybe not quite invisible.
She slammed the door behind her and walked down the
path removing the wheelie bin that her next door
neighbour Mr. Wilson had placed in front of her gate.
Her thoughts were at the very mundane tasks she had for

1

the day, not counting the mother and toddler session at the
   library.
She loved the session with mums chatting and the children
   shouting out at the pictures she held up in the books.
She felt alive which is more than could be said for the
   rest of her miserable life. From the outside people would
think she had quite a good life. Nice semi, husband,
   two grown up children, a very good job with the
   council library, a holiday now and again, what more
   could anybody ask for? She started to pick out the
   sentences, nice semi, yes but she had to care for her
   husband's mother who had taken residence in their
master bedroom. She lived next door to the most
   obnoxious man, who would leave rubbish outside
   their house, play loud music at night and allow his dog
   to leave piles of shit on the front lawn. Husband, now
   that was something else. He had been made redundant
   five years ago and had not worked since. He spent most
   of his days in front of the television, he had promised
   to do the nursing and care of his mother but that had
   not happened. He just watched Storage wars, any fishing
   programme or Alaskan Men living off grid. Jeff sat in
   his armchair surrounded by his things. Jeff's island
she called it, toothpicks, remote control and an array
of foils off his pills. He needed the pills to assist with the
   pain he had from his bad back, apparently the reason he
   could not find another job. Heathers children now grown
   were living on the other side of town. Tom, the eldest married
   with no children, she rarely saw him maybe once a month
   when he called in to see his dad. Claire their daughter,
   separated from her husband, called much more often with
two of the most spoiled children she had ever met. They
   didn't speak but held electronic games grunting when asked any
question, they didn't like any of the food Heather made
   and often came with a McDonald's happy meal.

Claire was unhappy with her lot and ensured everyone knew about it;
"But dad I haven't any money, I don't know what am I going to do?" Claire would whine.
Jeff would fold a twenty pound note up and press it into Her hand. Heather never knew why, Claire had a very good job with social services and more likely as not earned far more money than they had coming in. Every Sunday Heather would cook the lunch while Charlie 12 and Luke 10 sat with their 'IPads' or 'Game Boys', Jeff Watching yet another episode of Storage Hunters and Claire sprawled out on the sofa ."You are so lucky mother No worries with dad's redundancy sitting in the bank and your salary", Said a bored Claire Little did she know that Jeff had spent most of his Redundancy money.
A large flat screen television filled most of the lounge and Jeff had given Tom £5000 to help set up his and Sarah's Floristry business. Jeff just said, you can pay it back when you are able, there had never been any repayments made into the very sorry looking bank account. If it hadn't been for her job they would be in financial straits, though Jeff would never admit it. She arrived at work, as key holder she had to be there before the other staff arrived, she picked up the post and went to the kitchen to fill the kettle.
"Morning Heather" said Sharon and Christine
"Morning Pam"
"Morning"
All the staff present and correct.
Heather had worked at the library for 20 years, Staff Had come and gone but the latest had been there a couple of years and they all got on. The mother and toddler group started at 10.30am. Heather, as library supervisor took on this task and she loved it.
The mothers started arriving at 10.15 Heather noticed one of the mums, Tracy ,had a large black eye

baby Liam was sat in his pram with a bottle of what looked
Like cola.

"Oh that looks nasty Tracy" said Christine

"Oh this yes, I hit it on the wardrobe when I was getting
My clothes out, it doesn't hurt"

She touched the angry looking swelling.

"Once upon a time"

Heather started her story. Just before Heather had finished
there was a musical interruption and Tracy put her mobile
to her ear..

"Sorry Tracy no mobiles please" said Heather, Tracy blushed
and put her phone into her pocket. When Heather had
finished and cleared her books, she watched the mums
wheel their buggies into the High Street.

As Tracy left there was a tall scruffy looking man about
25 years old waving his arms in Tracy's direction. He grabbed
the girl and shook her. Heather put her hand to her mouth
what on earth....

Tracy pulled herself free and they walked off together. You
shouldn't get involved in other arguments Heather thought.
But she couldn't get the image of Tracy's' skinny little body
leaving the floor as the thug shook her.

CHAPTER TWO

At five o'clock Heather walked down the High Street. She realised that no one looked at her as they had done when she was younger and life shone out of every part of her body. The light had gone out. That's when she had started to disappear. Faces passing by with no acknowledgment that she belonged to the human race. As she crossed the main road and down towards her home, she passed the Three Cups public house where a group of young men and girls were smoking outside. Tracy was sat on a wooden bench with baby Liam still clutching his bottle of cola and at the side of her was the man or the boyfriend thought Heather. He was laughing out loud, joined by a chorus of hoots. They held bottles of beer and seemed to be having a good time. Tracy wasn't. She sat looking very sad, Heather wondered if they have been there all day and if that baby had been fed. She shouldn't get involved, it wasn't her business but the look on Tracy's face was enough to make Heather think that the girl felt just the way she did, insular, looking out on the rest of the world, a world that had forgotten them. Heather got to her front gate, the wheelie bin was gone but on the front lawn there was a large mound of dog crap. Shit.

The television was blaring out and Jeff didn't even turn around.

"What's for tea? We have visitors." Heather walked into the lounge, Claire was curled up at the top end of the sofa with Charlie and Luke squeezed on the other end, heads deep into their IPads.

"Hi Mum, had today off so I've been shopping and thought we would give you a nice surprise".

"Lovely" said Heather, "has anyone been upstairs to see granny?"

"Yes I've taken her a cup of tea", replied Claire "she says she wants fish for tea and she doesn't want it in batter."

Heather went upstairs to tell her mother in law that she hadn't brought fish. She must have climbed these steps a million times that week.

She went to the kitchen to prepare tea. When it was ready she dished it up, Jeff ate his in front of the television as Robson Green was fishing off Iceland. The children turned their noses up at the shepherd's pie and both announced they didn't like peas. Claire helped herself to a large plateful and went to watch Robson cast from a small dinghy.

Heather sat in the kitchen thinking about Tracy, that thug must have hit her, that's where the black eye had come from, she hated men who abused women in anyway. She wondered if the baby was safe from the thug, surely Tracy wouldn't let that happen, or would she be able to prevent it?

Thursday came around quite quickly and Heather arrived at the Library earlier than usual. She resolved that if that thug of a man attacked Tracy she would intervene. Nothing would stop her. She didn't care if he shouted back, she would tell him what a bully he was and if he tried to hit her, she would call the police and have him arrested. Heather felt a flutter in her stomach. She hadn't had that flutter for such a long time. She was excited, yes excited.

"Are you ok Heather" asked Christine

"Yes I'm fine" replied Heather feeling herself flush.

"I can do story time if you like, if you're not feeling too good"

"I said I'm fine" insisted Heather

It was 10.20am when Tracy arrived, baby Liam was snuggled up in a dirty looking red blanket. He held on close to his bottle of cola in one hand and a sausage roll in the other.

Tracy looked terrible, her eyes had dark circles around them, the yellowing of last week's black eye was still evident and around her neck she had an angry looking red mark. She saw Heather looking at her and drew her scarf closer so as not to show her injuries.

"Can we all sit down please ladies?" Heather announced then told her story. Her stomach curdled, she could feel herself getting hotter. Something was going to happen she just knew it.

At 11.30am the young mums got their things together and walked towards the door.

"I'm just going to get some fresh air Christine," Heather called to her colleague.

"Are you sure you are ok?" said a concerned Christine.

"I will be fine, honest" Heather gave her one of her motherly smiles.

Tracy was stood on the pavement looking up and down the High Street then out of the crowd came her boyfriend.

"Where the fuck have you been bitch?" he shouted, people turned around to sound of the profanities. Heathers heart jumped, this was it, she had to do something. Tracy and the boyfriend walked off, Tracy running a little to keep up with the long strides of the boyfriend.

"I fucking told you that I was meeting Kev why didn't you answer your phone?" the boyfriends face was red and his eyes were like saucers as he spat his sentence out.

"Sorry Scott, I am sorry they don't allow phones on in the library." she was almost begging him.

"You fucking will be sorry" he growled.

Heather found herself following the couple down the High Street she still didn't know what she was going to do. Her steps quickened as she tried to keep up, just far enough behind for them not to notice her. As they got to the large crossing she was herded among a crowd of other people to the crossing entrance. The lights were at red. Scott was still snarling abuse at Tracy as a Blue Western bus came out of the bus station and up the road. As it reached the crossing Heather pushed closer to the crowd. She could almost touch the couple. She pushed her body against Scott, he turned around and just had time to say," what the?," and he was gone. There were screams all around Heather, she looked at the body tangled in the front wheel of the bus, most people ran forward to where the body lay, Heather stepped backwards slowly at first then hurrying back to the library. As she went through the doors she could hear the sound of an ambulance and police sirens.

What had she done. Her heart was beating quickly as though it would burst through her chest, Christine was at the desk.

"Are you ok Heather, you look awful, are you ok ?"

"Yes I'm fine I think there must have been an accident at the crossing again I can see a bit of a crowd gathering."

For the rest of the day Heather waited for someone to come and arrest her but nobody did. She arrived home with three pork chops and a cabbage. Jeff was watching Pawn stars in Vegas, he had managed to create a pile of tobacco on the lounge carpet.

Heather swept the tobacco up tutting as she was doing it.

"Shut up woman tutting every two minutes don't you think I have enough going on here without you starting."

"There was an accident by work this morning" said Heather to an uninterested party.

"By the crossing, there seems to be one every week these days". Jeff grunted. She retired to the kitchen and cooked tea.

She helped her mother in law put on a clean nightgown and changed the TV channel so she was able to watch Coronation Street. Later that night Heather had a shower and got into the bed in the back bedroom. Jeff had been drinking and she didn't want to hear him snore. She laid still and looked up to the ceiling, she had killed someone, it had been frighteningly easy. No one had even looked at her, apart from the thug Scott. His eyes had met hers just for a second or two, he knew she had pushed him but now he couldn't tell anyone, he was dead wasn't he? No, he must be dead. He looked very dead. His head looked like a mashed turnip it wasn't a pretty sight all that blood..

Surprising herself Heather had a very good night's sleep. She got up at her usual time then prepared breakfast for her and Iris and left for work passing the hall mirror. She looked at the distant reflection of herself no change there then, disappearing by the day. At the bottom of the path she moved the wheelie bin and went into work.

A few people had come into the library that morning and told her of the terrible accident the day before. A poor young dad only twenty-four years old killed in front of his girlfriend and baby, it was so sad. Not if you had known him thought Heather.

"You look better today" said Christine," It's a wonder you didn't see that accident yesterday, I heard that it was the boyfriend of one of the young mums that come to our group"

" Oh no. Which one?" said Heather. Heather felt excited that she had told a lie and no one knew, although she still expected the police to come and arrest her at any moment; But nobody did.

A week went by, then two weeks. Heather read stories in the paper about the drug dealing of the deceased or what a devoted father the deceased was, such conflicting accounts but Heather knew the correct account. It didn't surprise her that he dealt in drugs or he prostituted his girlfriend, someone else also knew the true story.

Four weeks had passed and Heathers excitement had diminished she had returned to her mundane everyday life. It was Thursday and as usual the mother and toddler group, she saw Tracy from the desk she was dressed in a pair of new leggings and a black top she was pushing baby Liam who was clutching his bottle that looked as though it contained orange juice. What if she knows, Heather turned around and started piling books under the counter she had to calm down and not to give herself away. The mums settled down and Heather started her story. She cast the odd glance at Tracy to see if she had a flicker of acknowledgment. There was none. After the group had finished Heather went over to Tracy with Christine," We are so sorry to hear of your bereavement can we do anything to help"?

"No its fine I'm OK thank you" her voice was soft and educated not what Heather had expected, Tracy wheeled the pram out and onto the High Street.

CHAPTER THREE

In bed that night Heather thought again how easy was that. She remembered a character in the seventies on TV. What was his name? Yes, The Equalizer that's what she could be. Someone who extinguished evil, those people who did not deserve to be on Gods good earth. She smiled, yes Edward Woodward, The Equalizer she smiled again.

The next day as she set off for work the wheelie bin from next door had its contents spilled over the path and a large pile of dog mess mixed in. She could cry some mornings, why did he do it? She looked back at the adjoining house and Mr Wilson's face staring down at her. He was old but he was evil.

Heather spent the day at the library putting books back onto shelves she enjoyed this as she was always amazed by the books people would take out.

The book in her hand was of crimes that shook America, she glanced through the pages. There was a woman in Arkansas that had murdered eight husbands, she could do with murdering just one... and maybe his mother. She read down the page then over the next, the woman had used Rycin, a poison she had never heard of before. It came from the Castor oil plant. Mr Wilson had a large Castor oil plant in his garden it had giant shiny leaves she had always admired it. In fact, Mr Wilson's garden was very well cared for. Heather put the book back onto the shelf and thought.

Extreme fishing in South Africa was on the television and Jeff had just poured himself a large whiskey and coke.

"I'm off to bed" said Heather, no answer as the fisherman shouted "what a whopper" in the background.   Heather opened her laptop to poisons of the world and looked up Rycin. She felt that excitement in her stomach again.

Don't be stupid Heather, you will get caught she berated herself but this does look like it is the right tool for the job. She was interrupted by Iris who shouted that she would like a cup of hot chocolate. Heather made the drink and returned to the search for the good and bad points of killing someone with Rycin.

The next day she finished work early and walked down the High Street to the local market that was held every Friday afternoon. Next to the bus station there was still a sign propped up against the barrier. If anyone has any information as to the incident involving a pedestrian on 5th September 2014 please contact Bishop Horton Police 224488.

Heather didn't feel anything. She smiled and bought a pound of carrots. She then went to the makeup stall where the stall holder was tidying up the baskets that held colourful arrays of make-up. Heather picked a bright pink lipstick. Not her usual colour but she thought she would brighten herself up.

She held the lipstick and a five pound note up, the stall holder continued to fiddle with the make-up. A young woman stepped up to the stall and immediately the stall holder turned around and served her. Heather was furious, yes she was invisible, she put the lipstick down and returned the five pound note to her purse.

Sunday came, Claire and the children arrived for lunch, it went quite well as Claire sat with her Granny for most of the afternoon. Iris told Claire of times long past. The children didn't really bother with Iris, she wasn't part of the technical world and she smelt funny said Luke.

"I'm so tired" said Claire "we have been so busy this week I never have anytime for myself anymore."

Heather said, "Yes that is so important," but she knew what was coming.

"You couldn't babysit for me on Tuesday mum? I could do with a night out and the girls from work are going to Mario's for a meal."

"Of course she will" answered Jeff "we love having the kid's." Heather thought and when have you ever had them? In the past she would bake with them or colour but sadly as they had grown their interests had changed. The only thing they were interested in these days were their IPads.

"Yes sure, what time will you be home?"

"Shouldn't be later than 11.00pm" grinned Claire Heather nodded. The children didn't pay any attention.

"You couldn't have them after school too, I need to make myself look glamorous"

"Yes they can come here from school your dad will be in". Jeff's head spun around" Don't forget I have my mum to look after it can get a bit much you know."

Heather said she would book a day off and the children could come straight from school. Claire seemed happy to have a night out on the town.

Tuesday morning came and Heather welcomed the extra time in bed she got up about 8.00am and made tea for herself, Iris and Jeff."

The music from next door started. Mario Lanza just what she needed she made the beds, then took Iris her breakfast. She then went into the front garden and pushed Mr Wilson's wheelie bin back in front of his house.

"Don't touch my bin you bitch" screeched Mr Wilson.

"Please don't speak to me like that Mr Wilson its uncalled for"

"You stuck up bitch get back to your own house" he snarled

Heather was breathing through her nose and was trying to calm down. She had to remember he was an old man.

"You think you're so much better than anyone else don't you bitch" he screamed through the neatly cut privet hedge.

And up yours thought Heather.

Jeff was watching Wild in Alaska and rolling another cigarette. She went upstairs and gave her mother in law a cup of tea then went into the back bedroom. She started her laptop up and Googled Rycin. She read through the pages and pages of information. The children arrived with school bags and wants of crisps, chocolate and cola, Heather supplied all of the above it wasn't her place she thought of changing the habits of a lifetime.

Claire arrived home at midnight and was very drunk but wouldn't stay the night. Claire rang a taxi and went home, leaving the children fast asleep on the blow up beds in the dining room. Heather would have to get up extra early and make sure the children got off to school in the morning.

She got into the bed in the back bedroom and Googled Rycin again, it is a bit Scarpetta she thought after looking at the site of 10 poisons that are untraceable. The Internet was a world of wonder to Heather would you ever believe that there was such a site on the web. Heather wondered why there wasn't more murders about or maybe there was and were truly undetected.

Rhubarb leaves were very toxic but how was she going to get Mr Wilson to eat them. That was a little bit Agatha Christie chopping rhubarb leaves up and adding them to a salad... no that wasn't going to work. She hardly spoke to Mr Wilson never mind cook a meal for him. Then reality hit her in the face, she was thinking of killing someone, was she a monster? She had created an accident with Tracy's boyfriend. He did deserve it and Mr Wilson definitely deserved it. Scott had not directly hurt her, not as Mr Wilson had. Heather had spent many hours crying over the cruel ways Mr Wilson enjoyed getting under her skin.

She had spoken to Jeff about the dog crap and the wheelie bin and the swearing through the hedge.

Jeff told her not to be so sensitive. Mr Wilson was an old man and he had never had any trouble with him. Heather dropped off to sleep dreaming of collecting wild mushrooms and leaving them on the doorstep of Mr Wilson's house hoping he would make a soup out of them and dying a horrible death.

Heather slammed the door behind her and walked down the path removing the wheelie bin that belonged to her next door neighbour. Heather and the children walked down the High Street, the children taking the route for school and Heather going on to the library.

At 10.30am Heather received a message that all staff should be in the office at 11.30am as the area manager would be calling. Rumours had been going the Council offices that there were to be redundancies throughout library services. She was worried. What would happen to her she was almost sixty. She would never get another job she would have to be at home with Jeff and Iris. Oh my god she thought.

Nikki Farmer the area manager came to deliver bad news. The Council would be looking for redundancies in the area but she couldn't say just where they would be. All the staff were visibly upset; the library was a good place to work they all got on well together. Heather had worked there for 20 years she was part of the furniture. Why did they do this to people, mess their lives up she was angry and upset. All her plans for retirement the travelling the hobbies she could take up, gone in a five-minute statement and just look who was delivering it, a thirty something who was going places that was obvious by the power suit the high heels and the bright red lipstick. Nikki Farmer had been a part time library assistant only two years ago and here she was area manager of Bishop Horton Town Library services.

"Heather are there any questions", Heather almost jumped out of her skin as the words interrupted her thoughts.

"No, no, I'm fine we can only wait and see can't we. There is no reason to get too anxious yet is there?"

Nikki stared at Heather she could never understand this woman. Heather was always quiet, well-mannered but there was something Nikki couldn't put her finger on.

"Well that's me finished if you would rather speak to me in private about anything we have spoken about today please don't hesitate to get in touch, you all have my number. I am sorry I am the bringer of bad news."

Heather watched as Nikki's slim body manoeuvred around the desk and picked up her smart leather briefcase.

"Thank you ladies" and with a waft of Channel 19 she went. The other staff sat stunned, Christine started to cry,"

" I need this job what am I going to do?" Christine sobbed into her tissue.

"Come on Christine" said Heather we don't know what is going to happen let's just wait and see."

"How can you be so calm Heather" but Heather wasn't calm she was angry, very angry.

Heather just kicked the wheelie bin from the front of the path. There was knocking from the window above and Mr Wilson put two fingers up and mouthed bitch. She slammed the front door so hard Jeff asked what was wrong, nothing, she said only next doors bin again. She couldn't hear what Jeff's answer was and she wasn't going to tell him what had happened at work, there was no reason to start the constant nattering about what was happening.

She had a late start the following day Christine was opening the library and she didn't have to start until 10.30am. Heather made sandwiches for Jeff and Iris's lunch and covered them with foil she took her mother in law a large mug of tea, she placed a cup of tea on Jeff's table his gaze didn't move from Alaskan railway and she left the house.

Mr Wilson's dog had left his usual morning present on the front lawn. Heather took a plastic bag from her handbag and picked it up she walked to the side of the house to deposit the offending material into the bin. She heard a slight groan so she followed the sound. It was coming from the other side of the hedge she craned her neck around the edge where the houses adjoined, it was Mr Wilson he was laid on the ground his feet sticking out on the lawn she opened Mr Wilson's front gate.

"Help, help me, help me, my heart," stuttered Mr Wilson

"Well you're in a bit of a pickle" she knelt down by the side of Mr Wilson's body, did you want to say something to me Mr Wilson", the old man looked into Heathers eyes,

"You bitch" he muttered

"Well maybe I am or maybe I'm not," Heather spun on her leather Lotus kitten heels, shut the garden gate and carried on to work. She gave her colleagues a large smile as she entered the library.

CHAPTER FOUR

Claire had been asking Heather to babysit more frequently. Heather guessed she might have a boyfriend, although she thought Claire might have had more sense after the last marriage and bitter divorce.

"Hi Mum can you babysit Saturday night please?" asked Claire she was so bright on the telephone.

"Yes ok" answered Heather "make sure they bring the chargers for their IPads."

The children arrived with overnight bags and sulky faces they didn't like it at grandmas and granddad's house on the weekend because granddad always wanted to watch fishing, they had been bribed this time with McDonald's and milkshakes.

Next day Heather made lunch and Claire had arrived on time for once, she was very happy and joked with Jeff and the kids.

At the table Luke let the cat out of the bag,

"Mums got a boyfriend Gran, Claire glared at Luke.

"Oh that's nice" said Heather.

Claire smiled it was out in the open, "they call him Mike and he has an IT company you know doing web pages and such"

"Does he get paid well" said Jeff "Not like the other waste of space".

"Dad stop, the kids." Claire rebuked.

"How old is he" asked Heather

"He is 42 never been married no kids, which is a relief"

Heather was pleased she was happy it was easier for everyone.

"Why don't you invite him for Sunday lunch next week Claire it would be nice if me and your dad and Granny met him." Claire smiled, "Yes I will, I will give you a ring tomorrow to confirm. He is going to take me and the kids to the pictures on Saturday, Jurassic Park I think," both children shouted yeah.

In bed that night Heather felt happy things were going well for Claire and the kids, she then thought of Claire's ex-husband who had been very abusive even going to prison for the last horrific attack on her daughter. It was now 2 years after their divorce he stalked her at work left horrible messages on the phone and continued to be a pain in the arse, if she ever did plan a murder he would be the one to get it, not that she had murdered anyone, however there could be a first time, she opened her lap top and looked up Hemlock, the poisoners favourite, a good dose of Agatha Christie before she fell asleep.

Next day Claire rang as promised and said Mike would love to meet her parents and grandmother and looked forward to Sunday. Heather was content everything in the garden was rosy but of course that didn't last.

Nikki Farmer arrived from the Town Hall and said that after meetings with the unions and management they would be putting staff into consultation and everyone would have to apply for their own jobs, budgets had been cut but not enough. Heather was furious but did not show the distress she felt, Christine and other members of the team broke into sobs Nikki Farmer delivered her message with little emotion. After Nikki Farmer left Heather calmed her team down and everyone returned to work allowing the volunteers to go on their break. What is it with life just as you are getting up it kicks you in the teeth again?

When she arrived home Jeff was watching Deadliest Catch "what's for tea?" he asked

"Pork chops" she answered.

"Bloody hell Heather you know I hate pork"

"You will eat it though" she said "It's cheaper than other meat and we need to watch the money with you not working and me possibly being made redundant."

Jeff's head turned quickly" being made redundant you must be joking,"

"Do I look as though I'm joking."

"Bloody hell where are you going to get another job at your age "he said

"Thanks" answered Heather and took herself into the kitchen. That night in bed she wondered what she could do. Maybe she could put Hemlock into everyone's tea at work, then there wouldn't be a problem she had to have a little giggle to herself as she imagined the members of staff all sat around the staff room table dead and Miss Nikki Farmer announcing, as Heather was the only candidate the job was definitely hers and there would be someone from cleansing later to remove the bodies.

Next day the mood in the library was poor and she sent Christine out to buy vanillas to try and cheer everyone up.

"You will not have to worry Heather at your age I'm sure it will be cheaper to keep you working rather than them paying you off". Said Pam making a cup of coffee to go with the vanillas. Heather thought she could be right there, although she had a feeling that Nikki Farmer didn't like her for some reason but then again she didn't think she liked anyone.

On Thursday morning mother and toddler story time had started. Tracy wasn't there at the beginning. Heather had started reading Meg and Mog when the front doors of the library opened and Tracy walked in pushing baby Liam in his buggy, her face was grazed down one side and her lip had been burst at one point. Sorry I'm late she said and hurriedly sat in one of the bright orange chairs taking Liam from his buggy in one swift action.

Oh my God thought Heather she tried not to stare at Tracy in between pages. Tracy's hair was hanging down in greasy strands but it barely covered her cheek that clearly showed the shape of an iron.

Heather wanted to speak to Tracy after the story but Tracy bounced baby Liam into his pram and flew to the front door to avoid any contact with anyone. Heather followed her to the front door and stood and watched. No, No, Heather didn't know what to do there standing on the pavement outside was Sam (daughter Claire's ex-husband) he took the handles of the buggy and pushed baby Liam away down the High Street, Tracy had her head down and hurried behind him.

Heather couldn't believe her eyes when she saw Sam with Tracy what on earth would a young girl want with a monster like Sam. Heather remembered that Sam was a smooth customer he had charm and a vulnerable young girl like Tracy would easily be taken in by him.

CHAPTER FIVE

When Claire was younger she was a bit of a home bird. She didn't often go out with her mates she went to college and did well to become a social worker. That was where she had met Sam, he was at a case conference and asked her out. Claire was very shy, so it took Sam over a month before she agreed to go out with him. Then she was smitten, this lovely bloke bought her flowers, he wanted to meet her mum and dad it was a whirlwind romance. Jeff liked him, and had no hesitation in saying yes when Sam came to the house to ask permission for Claire's hand.

Claire sat in the kitchen with her mother so excited. Sam came back in with a cheesy grin, "come on I'm taking us all out for dinner". They spent the evening at the local Italian where they drank Prosecco and ate pizza. Those were happy times. Then the children came along their first grandchild she was beautiful lots of dark hair but what a name Charlie for a girl, Heather thought Ruth or Helen, no mother its Charlie. Two years following was Luke, he was a little cutie. Claire was going to take a year off on maternity then would go back part time with Sam's mother looking after the kids.

It was during this time that Heather noticed the odd mark on Claire's face, "what's wrong with your eye Claire?"

Claire put her hand to the injury above her eye, "Oh I was looking for something under the

dressing table and got up quickly and banged my face."
Another time was when Claire tried to help bring
Heathers shopping in from the car she couldn't hold
the bag as she was experiencing a lot of pain in her
arm and finger, the finger looked broken".

"They can't do anything at the hospital mum
probably just strap it up."

"Come in I will do it' Heather tied two fingers
together to give the little finger some support, "There
you are, are you going to tell me the truth now,
quizzed Heather.

"What do you mean truth, I don't understand"

"Truth about why you are having so many
little accidents, Claire tell me the truth I am your
mother.'

"Oh mum she flung her arms around her
mother. "it's Sam he says I am not paying as much
time as I should be with him and I always put the kids
first, not being there for him. He used to be so kind
and thoughtful, I am walking on egg shells constantly,
he just flares up. I know the job is tough and
policemen have a rough time but I am there for him."

"There, there' Heather patted Claire's head as
she sobbed herself out.

Heather couldn't let Sam get away with
hurting her daughter. She had to confront him it was
no use Jeff doing it they would just end up getting
pissed together. Jeff would then join in with Sam
saying that Claire deserved it.

Heather didn't want to go to Claire's house
so she found out from Claire what shifts Sam was on.
Sam was on duty the following ten o'clock am until six
in the evening. At eleven thirty the next the morning
Heather told Pam she was going on first lunch. She
walked down to Bishop Horton Police station and
asked for Sam. Sam came to the front desk all smiles,

Heather smiled back "can I have a quick word with you in private Sam?'

"Of course mother in law" he led her into a side room there were large posters on 'DOB in a dealer' and numbers for the local ombudsman.

"What can I do for you Heather, what's up?" He seemed so light hearted surely he couldn't have attacked her daughter. "It's Claire Sam, she seems to be having a lot of accidents recently I wondered if you knew anything about it"

"I hadn't noticed' he stuttered

"The black eye, the broken finger. you didn't notice?'

"Well I saw them but I don't know the details you have got to admit it Heather she is clumsy"

Yes, she was thought Heather she smiled at Sam "Sam I just wanted to say that if you ever do anything to hurt my daughter I will kill you. Do I make myself clear?" Her voice didn't fault, she didn't raise her voice as she delivered her message with steely grey eyes.

"Heather you shouldn't go around making those type of threats it could get you into a lot of trouble. Claire needs to be looking after me as her husband and to stop nagging me every two minutes. She is the one that lashes out, I just try to protect myself. So instead of coming here and giving me a lecture go speak to your daughter". Sam got up from his chair and left the room.

Heather felt hot and it was difficult to breathe, he had hurt Claire she could see it in his eyes, the bastard. She needed to keep a close eye on this situation.

The violence increased and on a couple of occasions Claire turned up in the middle of the night with the two children wrapped in blankets. Heather put the children to bed then sat with Claire as she nursed a cup of coffee her hands were trembling, "he is a pig mother, a pig'

"What's happened?" questioned Heather

"He came home after his shift, threw the supper I had made him in the bin then said he was going out with lads from Blue watch. He came in drunk and started saying I was a useless wife I didn't provoke him mum honest I didn't. He was so angry I got frightened so when he went to sleep on the sofa I got the kids into the car. I can't go back I can't.'

"You don't have to love you stay here." Heather enclosed her in the loving arms giving her a hug only a mother can give.

Claire and the children stayed for two days then Sam arrived at the doorstep with a large bunch of flowers for Claire and a bottle of whiskey for Jeff. Claire played hard to get, it was almost half an hour before Sam was helping to pack her things into her car.

"She will be alright Mother in law promise' he smiled the smile of the devil. Heather didn't smile back.

Jeff sat in his chair and said "Thank god for that I can get back into the bathroom again." Heather raised her eyes to the ceiling.

The second time Claire arrived she didn't have the children she was hysterical that she had had to leave them but it was the only way she could get out. To the side of her head there was a large gash that needed stitching, "we need to go to the hospital Claire,"

"No mum I can't go, my job, Sam's job.'

"But it's your life Claire, this man is going to kill you, what did he hit you with?

Claire sobbed "the rolling pin I only said he would have to wait for his shirt ironing as I was making biscuits with the kids"

"He did this in front of the kids?" Heather was shocked.

"Yes' said Claire as she bowed her head, "I'm frightened for the kids mum what am I going to do?"

"Well first things first we are going to the hospital to get your head sorted out then we are going to the police"

The hospital stitched Claire's head they also called the police when it was explained what had happened. Claire knew the police woman who came to the call she said that her and Sam had had a disagreement and she didn't want to cause a fuss she was worried about the children. The policewoman, Claire and Heather went to Claire's house the light was on in the kitchen, Sam was sat in the dark in the lounge. When he saw Claire he jumped up.

"Oh I'm so sorry Claire that should never have happened I'm so sorry." He put his arms around Claire and sobbed into her blood stained tee shirt'

"Sam I need to take a statement from you and your wife said the policewoman, "you hurt her Sam look at Claire"

"I know, I didn't mean to do it there's this case I'm working on it is very traumatic."

Claire turned to the police officer, 'it's okay nothing to report I will be fine.'

Heather stood up, "no Claire you must tell the officer what has happened'

"It's okay mum I over reacted. I'm fine" Heather knew that nothing she said would change matters she would find her daughter dead one day, murdered by her own husband.

Sam was very abusive eventually being imprisoned for 6 months after attacking her in front of the children. This was two years ago, since then he had stalked her at work, sent messages to her house phone, managed to get numbers to each mobile through friends and family. Sam had been a policeman in nearby Mapplebeck but had been sacked after being found guilty of the assault of Claire, although he had been assaulting her for years.

Claire had reported the assaults on herself on many occasions but Sam had always managed to talk himself out of any action. Claire was arrested on one time although she was soon sent home to experience another beating. Heather could never understand how or why Claire would stay with such a monster and subject her children to such sights.

Sam was always dressed to perfection, smart as a button he spoke well and on the outside a perfect husband and father. In reality he was a bully and control freak. To Heather and Jeff, he was the perfect gentleman he would say to Heather "why can't your daughter cook like you?" Heather would smile and blush Claire would glare. Sam would bring Jeff a bottle of whiskey, just to cheer him up. Jeff liked him, he was a man's man went to football talked about rugby and loved fishing just like Jeff. When Heather told Jeff about the abuse he wouldn't believe it. Claire was such an obstinate little mare it didn't surprise him, she was just like her mother.

However, Jeff did have to realise the truth when Claire had to be hospitalised. Her arm had a bad break she had two black eyes a broken jaw, a fractured skull and broken ribs. Sam had taken her to the hospital and this time there was a doctor who knew she couldn't have received the injuries that she had by falling down the stairs. Police were again called and the substantial injuries could no longer be passed over as a tiff between a married couple. Claire didn't even have to beg police officers to believe her.

Sam was arrested and no amount of pleading was going to restore this wrong. At court Sam turned up dressed in an immaculate grey suit, white shirt and grey tie he looked a professional gentleman. Claire held her mother's hand until she was asked to give evidence she was shaking, the bruises were still yellow and the arm that had been shattered was in its third cast. Sam explained that Claire had been nagging him about his job, he loved being a police officer. He was a respected member of the community with ten years' exceptional service. He had two bravery awards saving a small child from a kidnap situation also disarming a man with a knife. His wife wanted him to leave the force that he loved and do some boring job with the council he just flipped he saw red he wasn't that sort of guy to hurt his family.

Claire bowed her head as she stood in front of the judge and jury, she dare not look in the direction of Sam. She told the court that she had been assaulted throughout her marriage it had started when she became pregnant with her first child. Sam would get angry if things were not just right at home or if work had gone badly. She had rung the police on a number of occasions but nothing was ever done because Sam had talked his way out of any actions

The defence team painted Claire as a pathetic woman who wanted to control her husband. She had nagged and badgered him for months wanting him to leave the job that he loved. Claire said quietly that that was not true. The argument had started when Sam had said he was working another weekend and they had promised to take the children to Alton Towers he had cancelled it on three previous occasions she asked for just a weekend a month but Sam wasn't to be controlled.

Sam had grabbed her hair and punched her to the ground she said that she couldn't remember much more only that her hand had hurt then she was in the car going to the hospital. What Claire didn't know was that on punching her to the ground he had kicked her in the ribs breaking three, punched her again and again in her face he then picked up a table lamp and smashed her arm again and again as she tried to reach out.

The court case took four days, then the jury went out they were out for just two hours then brought in a guilty verdict. Claire sobbed into Heathers coat sleeve as Sam stared at Claire and he mouthed 'just wait'. Sentencing was two weeks later Claire didn't go however Heather did. The judge gave Sam 6 months and took his exceptional police record into account. The judge said that he had to give Sam this sentence because of the severity of the injuries but understood that it was in a circumstance that Sam had been under extreme pressure from Claire. Sam would pay the price of losing his job therefore the sentence was fitting.

Heather was shocked 6 months for almost killing someone, how could that be right he would probably only do two months inside. It would not be any easy situation as she had heard that when prisoners found out that he was a former police officer he would have a tough life in there. Sam bent his head then looked across at Heather and nodded, she wanted to stab him and crush his skull as he had done to Claire. But Claire would be safe for while in the meantime they needed a plan, Claire had to move house, move closer to her and Jeff.

So that's what happened. Claire took a rented house close to Heather and Jeff and resumed her work as a social worker and enjoyed not having to live the life of an abused woman.

Although Sam was in prison it didn't stop him from trying to contact Claire. She received letters at her mother's address every week from Sam first claiming his undying love for her, then veiled threats of what he was going to do to her for divorcing him. Claire read every letter, Heather had wanted to destroy them but Claire wouldn't let her, she said she needed to be reminded how evil he really was.

Just twelve weeks later Sam was released on license it was then that Claire's car started to be damaged, tyres slashed, large scratch marks on the paint work. Claire reported them all to the police but there was no evidence that Sam had done it .

Claire panicked immediately but Heather told her the law was on her side and that if he contacted her the police would pick him up and send him back to prison. Claire was not convinced and stopped with Heather for a week. Claire wasn't happy having to help out with Iris so made an excuse that the children wanted to return to their home with all the electronic gadgets.

Claire returned home and everything was quiet for a month or two then the phone calls started again, she had pizzas delivered, wreaths, taxis at all times of the day and night. One morning she got into her car and scratched on the windscreen was 'Bitch'. Claire rang her mother who then advised her to ring the policeman and appointment was made for later the following day.

The two uniformed officers who interviewed Claire didn't seem to take her complaint seriously. They asked if she had fallen out with neighbours she said not and that it was her ex-husband but they already knew that thought Claire.

"Why would you think it was your ex-husband?" asked the female officer.

"He has a history I am sure you are aware?" snapped Claire.

"What evidence do you have Mrs Grey?" asked the other officer.

"I don't have any" a defeated Claire answered.

"I have lived here for only three months I have never met my neighbours apart from nodding and saying good morning. Claire knew this was a waste of time.

"I'm scared," Claire whispered "I'm frightened for my children".

The officers said they would investigate further and suggested Claire install CCTV it would make her feel safer and they would be able to gather evidence of the perpetrator.

After the installation of the cameras there were no further incidents so Claire came to the conclusion that it was a disgruntled neighbour after all.

CHAPTER SIX

Tracy thought about the day Sean had his accident. The crowd behind them at the crossing surged forward just as the lights were changing. She looked into his eyes just as the bus screeched and ran over his head squashing it flat to the road. One of his eyes blinked then popped out of its socket. She could hear screaming all around her. She didn't scream she stared at the lifeless body of the man she shared a bed with. She was taken from the scene in a police car. Baby Liam was fastened tightly into a car seat beside her. When they reached her flat the policewoman held Liam. The policeman put his arm around her and led her to the front door.

"Are you sure you don't want us to get someone to sit with you. Your mum a neighbour or any other family member?"

"No" said Tracy" I haven't got anyone now." She burst into tears and held the PC with both hands. Things had been hard Sean had always sorted their benefits out he had done the shopping told her what to do, what on earth was she going to do.

During the week her neighbour Sally called in to see her. Tracy liked Sally but couldn't make friends with her before as Sean wouldn't have liked it he said she was a 'scrubber' always out drinking, a smack-head.

Tracy didn't think she was a smack-head as she knew so many of Sean's friends to be one.

"Hi Tracy I've just come around to see if you're ok how you doing?" Sally was so chirpy.

Tracy answered that she was alright she invited Sally in for a cup of tea.

"Oh you don't need that muck, hang on," Sally shot out of the flat and returned to Tracy's door carrying a bottle of White lightening Cider.

"This will be better come on girl you need a break."

The two girls drank the two litre bottle in no time, crying, laughing in turn as baby Liam played on the carpet with a spoon and cup then falling asleep on the rug.

Sally started calling regularly to Tracy's house and the girls struck up a friendship.

"You need to get out of this flat girl why don't we go out this Friday. Its pay day so we can spend a little we might get some bought if we are lucky"

"What about Liam I can't leave him." Said Tracy.

"Don't worry my sister is fourteen she will baby sit she will do it for a couple of quid."

"I, I don't know Sally I haven't anything to wear" stuttered Tracy.

Sally laughed out loud, "Where do you think we are going I'll help you with some makeup your jeans look ok. I have a top you can borrow. I'll get a bottle of Lightening before we go then we don't spend so much, go on live girl". Sally did a little dance in front of her and Tracy laughed.

Tracy was worried she hadn't been out for such a long time she didn't often go with Sean to the pub it damaged his street cred.

She thought it would be nice having a night out she was sick of the flat. "ok I'll go"

"Yeah that's my girl we are going to party, we are going to party. Sally danced around the room and Tracy joined in.

Friday night came and Sally's sister arrived at seven o clock with her mate and Sally.

"This is my sister Faith and her mate Danielle" said Sally who was kitted out in a pair of black jeans and a sequined top. Her face made up with carefully painted on eyebrows.

"Let's look at you then", Tracy had on a pair of clean blue jeans the second pair she owned and a white t shirt she had no make-up so Sally carefully painted her face.

"There you go; you look fab girl" said Sally as she stepped back to admire her handy work. While Tracy had been made up a bottle of cider had been shared around the girls they giggled constantly.

"Keep still you silly mare" said Sally as she tried to adjust the curved brow line.

Sally checked the brows again.

"Mm mm they are sisters but there not twins," she gave Tracy the mirror, she looked at herself OMG she didn't look too bad.

"Well you scrub up well come on or the pub will be shut."

Both women laughed down the stairs of the flats and their heels clicked on the pavement up to The Three Cups pub it was full inside the bar and Tracy and Sally squeezed through to the main bar.

"Two halves of cider, two pounds" said the barman.

"Tracy it's you, sorry about Scott we all miss him here."

"Oh thank you" Tracy's head bowed she hadn't expected anyone to know her. She didn't often go into the pub, she usually sat outside on the wooden benches with Liam in the buggy. She would sit there for hours sometimes without a drink while Scott drank pint after pint. Tracy didn't miss Scott now she was glad he was dead.

The music was loud in the pub and there was a crowd gyrating to the music of Lady Ga Ga. Sally and Tracy drank their cider in between dancing and laughing.

Tracy turned around and went to the bar to order another drink.

"I'll get those smiler. Tracy glanced at the dark haired stranger he was old she thought but not that old he seemed so posh he had lovely teeth all white and straight.

"No its ok I'll get my own" blushed Tracy.

"Oh an independent lady I like those", she smiled a shy smile. "Come on, no strings attached" he held both hands up. Tracy smiled back "oh go on then." He paid for the drinks and Tracy went back to Sally who now had her arms around a short ginger haired boy. Sally took the glass from her and drank the cider in one go. Tracy pointed to the dark good looking man in the corner of the bar and told her the drinks had been bought by him.

"Oh he's nice a bit old but scrummy go girl."

"I think I want to go now Sally, I don't know if Liam will settle"

"I'm not going yet its only ten o clock."

"Please Sally." Begged Tracy

The ginger haired boy groped Sally's chest, "ya cheeky bugger" said Sally and punched the boy in his face. The boy flung a punch back and caught Sally in the eye. Mayhem erupted in the pub as chairs glasses and handbags were thrown across the room. Tracy and Sally managed to get to the front door of the pub Tracy's head spun when the dark stranger stood at their side.

"Are you young ladies ok? I saw what happened do you need to ring the police or anything?"

Sally looked bemused, "no we are ok."

"Can I walk you home just in case the rabble follows, how about a curry I'll buy?"

"Of course we would love to." Said Sally

"I can't" said Tracy "I have to get back I have a babysitter; I have a baby."

"Well you would have if you've got a babysitter."

Sally and Tracy laughed she liked the stranger.

"Look how about I buy you both a take away, walk you home if you promise me a date"

Tracy stared at him.

"Of course she will" Sally shouted. Tracy smiled she felt special. They all walked to the local curry house and bought chicken curries. Jack walked the young women to the entrance of the flats.

"Good night ladies" Sally took the brown carrier and ran off up the stairs. Tracy faced Jack her heart jumped, "well do I get a date?"…oh a real date thought Tracy she had never been on a date before. When she met Sean it just happened they were part of a big group and just ended up together.

"Yes, I would like that" she blushed.

"I will meet you here on Sunday night" said Jack

"ok well I need to get a babysitter" they exchanged mobile numbers and Tracy dashed off up the stairs to eat her chicken curry.

The babysitters were paid and booked for Sunday she was happy the girls laughed, "did you kiss him then?"

"No I didn't" said a shocked Tracy.

"My god" said Sally "and he bought our supper you would have thought he would want a shag for that most others would."

Sunday came and Tracy got herself ready with Sally doing her make-up. Jack was waiting for her as arranged.

"You look nice," he said she grinned and felt like a princess he took her to a lovely pub on the other side of town.

"Have you had anything to eat?"

"Just a sandwich"

"Well let's eat here" said Jack. They both tucked into steaks and chocolate fudge cake. Jack asked so many questions about her life she told him about Sean and the accident and how she had no other family being brought up in care. Jack didn't tell her that much about himself he worked as a civilian in the police force doing CSI stuff on murders and accidents. He had been married when he was twenty but it hadn't worked out and he had been divorced by the time he was twenty-five they didn't have children although he would have liked them. His wife never did she was a career woman. Tracy saw he was still angry with his wife as he drew his brow together causing a scowl. They had a lovely evening and walked through town hand in hand. Tracy felt safe at last it was her dream come true he was a little older than her but she didn't care he was a good man good sense of humour and he had a job which had to be a bonus.

At the entry to the flats Jack lent forward and kissed her on her forehead. She looked back at him thinking that he wouldn't want to meet her again most men or boys would have grabbed her by now. "You're so lovely Tracy can I meet you again? He whispered.

"Yes, yes" she said, this time he bent her head and kissed her so softly she felt as though she would fall over. They arranged another meeting later that week she said that she couldn't afford another babysitter so Jack said that he would pay the fiver. He had to meet with her again.

That night Tracy dreamed of wedding dresses and bridesmaids. For the following weeks they met up regularly. Jack sometimes was a little late but she understood, he had been at a scene of crime that had to be processed that day. He was so intelligent she thought why would he want to be with a simple sort of girl like her. She said this to Sally who was feeling a little left out, older men like young girls it makes them feel good and if his posh wife was one of these career women he might want someone more homely. Tracy didn't know if that was a compliment or not.

Tracy introduced him to Liam after a few weeks Liam loved the attention Jack showed him Tracy thought he was a natural father.

"You are so good with him" she said "it's as though you have done this before."

Jack laughed "I wish." Tracy wanted to be with Jack all of the time and it was discussed how they would take things forward.

"You could always move in here with me," said Tracy "It's quite a big flat."

Jack had said that he had a one room bedsit after the divorce and had not moved on from there. She hadn't been to his place but she understood men's places were not always that nice.

Jack thought about the move to her place for almost an hour then agreeing as he also wanted to be with her he thought they should think about getting married and having a family of their own. Tracy's dream was coming true she was blissfully happy. The following week Jack arrived in a taxi with a number of bin bags and boxes. Tracy had moved her clothes out of a set of drawers and Jack put his very neatly ironed clothes into them. They rang the local take away to celebrate.

"I hope you can cook" he said "we can't be living on take aways we need to save for our house." Tracy thought about the prospect of a large kitchen and a garden for Liam to play in, sheer bliss.

Tracy couldn't remember the exact day but she remembered the time it was 8.00am and she had quietly slipped out of bed to get Liam's breakfast. Jack was sound asleep at the side of her he wasn't working that day as he was on night duty. She crept into the back bedroom and took Liam out of his cot, she laid him in front of the television while she made a bottle for him and a cup of tea for herself. Walking into the lounge Liam's eyes lit up to the sight of the freshly made bottle she swept him up and plonked him down on her knee.

The baby eagerly drank the baby formula she hummed a little tune, "Tracy, Tracy" Jack shouted.

"I'm feeding Liam" she answered.

"Tracy come here" Jack shouted again.

"I'm feeding Liam love I'll be there in a minute" men they are so impatient. Then it happened so fast a sharp slap to the side of her face.

She lost her hold on Liam who fell to the floor but she still clutched the feeding bottle, Liam screamed at the impact.

"You ignorant bitch didn't you hear me I need a drink too, I work day and night for you two and nothing in return"

"I'm sorry Jack I would have made you one when I had finished feeding Liam" she was still in shock.

"So I'm last on the list again"

"No Jack no but the baby needed feeding." Her stomach was rolling over and over she was going to be sick. Jack mumbled and went into the kitchen to make a cup of tea. On returning to the lounge Tracy was hunched up close to a pink furry cushion, what had just happened.

"I'm sorry Tracy" he said and knelt in front of her stroking her hair "work has been a bitch this week but I'm doing it for us we have had a terrible murder case I'm so sorry you know I love you".

She knew he did and kissed his forehead, "its ok I understand sorry, I should have come into you to see if you needed a drink."

They cuddled and things settled down you have to expect him to be edgy because of the job he did. He worked so hard most of his wages were put into savings for their new house and they existed on Tracy's benefits with Jack helping out with bills here and there.

Sally didn't go around to Tracy's very often Jack didn't like Sally he thought she was a bit of a tart. Tracy was far too good to be with someone like her. But when Jack went to work Tracy would send her a message to come around for half an hour they often shared a bottle of white lightening and had a giggle. As weeks went on the violence increased she had told Jack to leave but he always managed to talk her around. He loved her she knew and they had a dream together.

Tracy's life was going down in a spiral. They very rarely went out Jack wanted to save as much money as possible so they had to make sacrifices. Jack was very good in other ways he would do the shopping for her so she didn't have to bother. He started to take Liam to the doctors or to see the nurse so she could have a rest he was very caring. But it was his temper it was a lot like Sean's but with Sean you could tell when he had lost it and you always knew when he would kick off. Jack was more sophisticated he often went quiet then would watch her every move then it was as if something or someone had pressed a red button to trigger something in his head and he had to lash out.

Jack would often be quiet for lengths of time which frightened Tracy she felt like a cat on a hot tin roof expecting something to happen.

She told this to Sally in confidence over a beaker full of white lightening.

"I know he works hard and we are saving so hard for a new house." Confided Tracy.

Sally thought for a moment then had a gulp of the cider.

"He sounds like a physco to me, get shut of him Tracy you had enough with the last one. If any man did anything to me I would knock his fucking head off".

They both burst out laughing as Sally did her kung Foo impression. The door opened and in walked Jack he was dressed in dark blue jeans and a black tee shirt.

"Well ladies you seem to be having fun what's going on?" he smiled at Tracy and Sally.

"Oh you know just having a laugh" Sally said "I'm off then let you two love birds get on".

The door of the flat closed with a bang. Jack picked up the television remote. Tracy felt nervous she had seen that look before. Without looking at her Jack snarled "I thought I told you not to have that tart in here,"

"She just popped around to say hello,"

"She just popped around to say hello" he mocked in a high pitched voice, "you pathetic bitch I am working my balls off and you're here getting pissed what sort of mother are you, what sort of wife would you make."

"I`m sorry Jack" she lowered her head as though bowing to him. He switched the television on to the news.

"I need a clean shirt for tomorrow I suppose you haven't done that either?".

"I'll do it now no problem" she got the ironing board out and plugged the iron in to the socket
"Are you stupid, move it out of the way of the telly."

Tracy took the ironing board into the kitchen and started to iron a crisp white shirt she put it onto a hanger and hung it on the curtain rail in the living room.

Jack looked up, "about time."

"Have you got a meeting tomorrow Jack?" Jack didn't answer" I just wondered if you could get me some money. The electric will run out tomorrow, Ten pounds would be enough."

"If you weren't partying all night with your mates it would have lasted a lot longer"

"I wasn't partying Sally only came around to see if I was alright." It just popped out of her mouth she knew she shouldn't have said anything but it was too late Jack twisted in his chair. She ran towards the kitchen door whimpering as she went. As she reached the door she felt Jacks hand grab her hair. He twisted her hair around his fist and pulled drawing her close to his snarling face.

"You cheeky bitch what's wrong with you, will you never learn I fucking told you about that tart you are all the same" with that Jack picked up the unplugged iron and slammed it into her face Tracy screamed in agony.

"No Jack please no" she screamed again as he punched her in her stomach she fell to her knees crying. Jack stood over her his breathing was fast and hard.

"You made me do that Tracy I didn't want to do it, you made me do it" he sat on the floor at the side of her and started to cry she raised herself to her knees and put her arms around him.

"Don't cry Jack I'm sorry don't cry."

In the bathroom Tracy looked at her face you could see the shape of the iron on her cheek it was red and angry and blisters were appearing already. How on earth did she get herself into this situation again. She knew Jack loved her and his job was so high pressured she needed to look after him better than she had been doing.

She wouldn't encourage Sally anymore she wanted to be a good wife have a nice house she had to try harder. She went back into the living room Jack had poured them both a glass of wine.

"Come on beautiful" he handed her the glass she held out a shaking hand.

"Cheers" said Jack and kissed the back of her hand.

Next day Jack didn't put the clean crisp white shirt on he put a black tee shirt and jeans.

"Change of plan chick I have to call into town first. Business you know, will you be going to your story time with Liam?"

"I don't want to go Jack" mumbled Tracy,

"Why not?" asked Jack Tracy's hand moved towards the blistered cheek. She had tried to hide the mark but it had been difficult with the blistering.

"I just don't feel like going", she didn't want people asking questions. Heather who took the story time always stared at her she would definitely notice her cheek.

"I insist you go" said Jack, "and I will meet you after and we can go to The Bluebird for a sandwich and a coffee". His smile always won her over but she still didn't want to go however she also felt the glint of steel in his eye she had to go.

"That would be lovely Jack" she got Liam ready and they both walked down the High Street, Tracy walking into the Library and Jack whistling away striding off to his business.

CHAPTER SEVEN

Sam never thought that he would be sent to prison. His colleagues at the station had spoken to him about the times they had been called to the house on a domestic. He had told them that Claire was a nag and was always complaining about him doing any overtime. She always had a bad temper and yes he sometimes reacted, what bloke wouldn't. The night of the big argument he couldn't really remember what started it off but it must have been something Claire had moaned about constantly. Yap yap in his ear. He just wanted her to shut up to keep her bloody mouth shut.

He remembered the kids coming down stairs when he had smashed her arm he had forgotten about them. They were crying he said mummy had fallen down the stairs. Charlie had already rung the ambulance she was a clever girl must take after himself. He needed a story but he didn't think about the police coming after the ambulance. It was one of his friends from Blue Watch the police officer just stared at the scene before him.

The policewoman took the children into the kitchen and that was it. He was taken to Bishop Horton police station they didn't put handcuffs on him which was a bonus. When he got to the station the desk Sargent was straight faced and he was taken into an interview room while a solicitor was sent for.

Colin his buddy sat beside him in the dank interview room.

"Sam what have you done, you have gone too far this time she is badly injured"

"It's not my fault Colin you know what she's like." Wailed Sam.

"Sorry you have gone too far" said Colin. Sam was bailed to his mother's house in the next town of Mapplebeck. He had to have no contact with Claire the children or any family member.

On the first day of the trial he entered the dock and saw Claire who sat close to her mother. Look at the state, he thought how did he know that she would still have to have a plaster cast on. Go on Claire wring it for all its worth. Claire wouldn't look at him but Heather, she stared back at him she had cold eyes they didn't really match her face he hadn't notice that before. Well the trial didn't go the way he expected the bitch lied through her teeth, although the judge was on his side he could tell and six months, well. Prison was hard the inmates knew before he arrived that he had been a copper so he was put in isolation that was ok he had no problem with his own company. He had to plan, Claire was not going to get away with this his career gone, his children gone, his house his car his mates everything gone. His mother was the only person to stick by him she knew he couldn't hurt anyone it wasn't in his nature.

Jack served eight weeks it was only a token gesture from the judge. He had played the system inside and he had to attend an anger management course. When he was released on license there was a condition he had to live at his mother's house. There was plenty of time to send letters to Claire from prison he tried to be as nice as possible as all mail was scrutinized but mentioning a few events in their sad lives to keep her on edge. He liked to think of ways to unsettle her so when he was released he bought a pay as you go phone then it couldn't be traced, he sent pizzas and wreaths to their old address. Claire then moved but that was easy enough to find he just rang the children's school said that they were moving as a family and gave them a false address the secretary then said that the address they had was *** and hey presto the new address.

Sam would walk past Claire's house at midnight usually the lights were out he left notes on her windscreen he slashed her tyres a couple of times. She would pay for what she had done. He had used his mother's car and sat in it all night on a couple of occasions he felt close to the children he missed them. On one of the nights he sat there he noticed a small red light in the eves of the house blinking softly. The sly bitch she had had CCTV installed got to give it to her that's just what he would have done.

Sam thought he would have to leave her alone for a while give her a false sense of security. He smiled to himself he needed to take a break. Sam went to The Three Cups public house. He remembered being there as a young lad having his first drinks with mates. The pub was full of bright young things moving with the beat of the music. He could not understand why the young woman had tattoos he wasn't that old but it was only men that had them when he was young. They dressed like tarts even the chunky ones had skirts up their arses. He saw Tracy when she first came into the pub she was taller than the girl she was with. She looked nervous of the crowd not like the other woman she was with who was now hooting and waving her arms above her head. Sam moved across the bar getting closer to the two young women. He smiled when Tracy came to the bar by herself. She had an amazing smile, he bought the drinks and introduced himself as Jack he thought he had better not give his real name, not yet anyway.

He felt a bit of a Don Juan as he smoothed his way into her life she was shy and vulnerable and was waiting for her knight in shining armour. He remembered the accident that had killed her boyfriend she told him about the abuse she experienced from him. Sam sympathized with her telling her that he would never hurt her. She lived in a block of flats close to the High Street. It would be ideal for him to live there he was getting a feeling of cabin fever. His mother fussed over him too much always asking where he was going, what did he want to eat, what time was he going to be home. So it wasn't long before he moved in with Tracy and baby Liam. The baby was ok quite content for the sad little life he had had so far. He had told her that he worked for CSI she just absorbed it all he had a little money from the sale of the house but not much. His probation officer a young kid in his twenties tried to get him to apply for jobs but no one would want an ex copper with a criminal record. He had told Tracy he would put all his money in the bank and they would live off her benefits. There was no point in declaring him living there messing all the money about they had to see if living together would work. He planted the seed of marriage and a house that's all most women would want and besides he was quite a catch. He didn't like the way Tracy had gotten close friends with Sally she was a nuisance and Sam had to tell Tracy he didn't like the way Sally was always hanging about she had got the message and Sally didn't call as much. If the bell went he always went to the door he would tell Sally that Tracy was sleeping or they were just about to go out she soon got the message.

He told Tracy that it was for the best, when they had their own house in a nice leafy suburb of Bishop Horton they wouldn't want Sally calling, then they would have friends who were somebody, other police officers or doctors or solicitors it would be best to break the tie now. Tracy was a little upset but understood where he was coming from. Everything in the garden wasn't rosy he had to chastise Tracy a couple of times. She would get on his nerves when she asked him where he was going and what he had been doing. She had to learn how to respect her partner the incident with the iron was unfortunate but she understood he was under pressure.

Sam had arranged to meet Tracy outside the library. He knew that Claire's mother worked there. He wouldn't go into the library but he would try to ensure Heather saw him and that he wasn't on the scrap heap. He had a beautiful young woman he had another family Claire hadn't taken everything away. He strolled up the High Street and waited outside the library he tried to peer into the large windows to the front of the building he could see a number of women sat in a circle then push their chairs away he saw Heather she looked just the same, a plain nondescript person dull inside and out so full of her own importance. Tracy walked towards the door pushing the buggy with Liam in she wasn't looking ahead but at the floor and Heather was following her just what he wanted, he put his arm around Tracy when she came out he could see

Heathers face out of the corner of his eye she was shocked he was sure she openly gasped, plan well executed.

CHAPTER EIGHT

Heather couldn't breathe. She stood and watched the couple push baby Liam down the High Street. Her heart was tearing in two. Heather didn't know what to do, did she tell Tracy, did she tell Claire. Her mind was so muddled the rest of the afternoon was a blur. She rushed home and spoke to Jeff who was watching Ice Road Truckers.

"I've just seen Sam, Jeff" Jeff turned his gaze from the television

"What where?" He looked confused.

"At the library he was with a young girl" she could feel her heart beating hard in her chest.

"What do you mean a young woman?"

"One of the young women that come to the story time with their babies, she must only be twenty-one or two what shall we do. Do you think we should let Claire know?"

"There is no point in upsetting her she doesn't care who he is with she has enough on her plate now."

51

That was it he turned in his chair and continued with his viewing. Heather was in turmoil she didn't know if she should tell Tracy. The girl had already experienced the brutality of the man he would never stop his violence Tracy had moved from one monster to another.

In bed that night she thought of the day she had pushed Sean in front of the bus. It had happened so quickly and he was snuffed out no longer able to terrorise a woman and baby. But if she hadn't done it Tracy would still be with Sean and not Sam what could she do? Heather had a bad night there were monsters in the bedroom she was stirring a giant cauldron adding eye of newt and wing of bat.

At work she looked through the files of the story time group where names and addresses were stored. Tracy lived in the flats close to the High Street she would walk that way at lunch time she didn't know what else to do. Lunchtime came and Heather told the other staff that she was going to do a bit of shopping and would see them later. She hurriedly crossed at the junction passed The Three Cups public house and on to the Flats. Grosvenor House was the end block of three. The number was fifteen so she worked out that that was the third floor. It was pretty quiet on this leafy avenue what was she supposed to do? There was a bench close by so she sat there gathering her thoughts. Just as she was about to go Tracy emerged from the entrance with baby Liam in his buggy she had her hair pulled up into a pony tail looking younger than her twenty-two years. Where was Sam had he got a job she doubted it who would employ such a waster. She decided to follow Tracy up the High street she may be meeting Sam, then what.

Tracy was walking quite quickly pushing the buggy swiftly over the curbs. Then Heather realised where she was going. She was going to the DSS office,

Heather wondered if Sam was living with Tracy this man was worse than Sean she suspected that he was and Tracy had not declared him or told the council that he was living with her. She could leave a message on the fraud line or even ring the council but Sam would know it was her but then again should she care. However she did care about Tracy in a funny way. She had put Sam into Tracy's life it was her fault that Tracy had suffered further abuse from this monster.

Heather returned to work. She worked all afternoon on the crime section putting books in alphabetical order of authors. She knew that she was going to have to get rid of Sam he deserved to die for what he had done to Claire and for what he was doing to Tracy he was worse than an animal. This was going to be difficult his death could not be traced back to her or have any connection with Claire. Tracy could not be involved as she already had one boyfriend dying from an accident she couldn't have another one going the same way, she may be arrested. Heather needed to find out what Sam was doing during the day. She had ten days leave to come she could take it next week and do a little detective work she felt pleased with herself to rid the world of Sam would be a joy.

CHAPTER NINE

The following week she didn't tell Jeff she was
on annual leave she wore the same grey skirt and white
blouse as she did any other work day. She left the
house at the same time and walked into town she sat at
the side of a large sycamore tree on the opposite side
of the avenue to Grosvenor House flats. She hoped
that she had not missed Sam. If Sam had a job he may
have left earlier. But at nine thirty the doors to the flats
opened and Sam strode out dressed in jeans and a
black tee shirt. He walked to the High Street and
stood at the bus stop. Five minutes later the bus for
Mapplebeck pulled up and Sam got on it. So he was
going to his mother's house probably not working
then only to be expected. She walked back to
Grosvenor House flats and sat on her bench by the
sycamore tree it was nice that the weather was
favourable as she sat in the sun trying to cook up a

plan for murder, yes murder, because that is what was going to happen.

Tracy didn't come out of the flats all day but at four o'clock Sam returned with a Tesco carrier. He walked down the avenue swinging the carrier as though he hadn't a care in the world. Unbeknown to him he had a major problem and that would be in the shape of his ex-mother in law Heather.

Tuesday morning Heather did the exact thing, leaving for work at the same time. She took up her place on the bench then at nine thirty Sam rushed out and ran up to the bus stop he jumped on the bus for Mapplebeck. What a good son he is, pity he wasn't a good husband and father. At four o'clock Sam returned as before not carrying anything this time. Heather went home to find Jeff watching Robson Green extreme fishing. Iris was settled watching Midsomer murders so she made tea and got her things ready for the next day. Wednesday morning, she sat on her bench by the sycamore tree Sam didn't come out at nine thirty as on the previous two days she wondered if Tracy was alright then at ten o'clock the doors opened to Sam, Tracy and baby Liam in his buggy. Sam was pushing the buggy as Tracy followed close behind. Awh, thought Heather it was market day. Heather guessed they would be going there and she was right. She followed close behind keeping her head lowered but just having them in sight. They moved slowly through the stalls buying vegetables and fruit just like any other normal couple would but Sam was not normal he was the scum of the earth. After shopping the little family returned to the Three Cups. Sam went inside and Tracy sat on the benches outside. After half an hour Sam came out and the trio walked back to the flats. Heather sat on her bench and waited it wasn't long before Sam came out he ran down the Avenue. Heather took after him as fast as she could reaching the corner of the High street. He was out of sight then as she turned the corner Sam stood in front of her.

"I thought it was you Heather, I don't suppose most people would take any notice of poor little nondescript Heather. What do you want mother in law, come to give me a warning what?" He snapped.

Heather wasn't frightened of him and he sensed this.

Through gritted teeth he said, "you saw me at the library didn't you. Well I'm back and you can't stop me from being in my own town."

"You need to leave Bishop Horton now Sam or I will tell Tracy all about you I don't suppose she knows your past." Reiterated Heather.

"Whether she does or doesn't has nothing to do with you, you and your idiot daughter are no longer in my life. Although I may have to pay a call on the lovely Claire. She hasn't done bad for herself lucky girl ehh! nice house on Waverly Gardens, nippy little Citroen and a new fella, although he looks a bit of a drip they must get on well together."

Heather was horrified he knew everything about Claire she wouldn't be safe from him he had to be exterminated.

"I'll go to the police you can't make threats to me." Said Heather boldly.

"What have I done, what have I said, nothing, I have a lovely young, yes young girlfriend. We are going to get married you are the one following me. I may have to have this conversation logged, stalking is a crime now you know." He smirked

Heather knew he was serious.

"Sam do not contact Claire or the children this is my only warning." Said Heather in a low steady voice.

"OH the woman has spirit I bet no one would reckon that from you, Mrs Nobody. Claire and I used to laugh at you in your grey skirt, grey hair, grey personality, Mrs Nobody.

Heather wasn't grey at that moment her cheeks were a very beautiful shade of damson her eyes shone like small diamonds. If she had had a knife she would have cheerfully stuck it into his ribs. The two starred at each other no other words passed their lips. Then Sam laughed and moved around her, back to Grosvenor House. Claire was in turmoil she watched him go swaggering down the street he had marked his card as her grandmother would say.

For the rest of the week she told Jeff that she had taken annual leave he had nodded then returned to Robson Green landing a sail fish in South Africa. Heather spent the rest of the week researching methods of murder she read a Lee Childs book, an Agatha Christie, James Patterson and an Ian Rankin, food for the soul.

Most of the books the murderer didn't get away with murder she had to and she didn't want Claire or Tracy to be involved or come under suspicion

Heather stayed awake most of the night trying to think how she would tackle the problem of Sam. In the early hours of the morning she had an idea.

Saturday morning Heather got up and took her shopper out of the garage and walked onto the market at one stall she bought a pack of small plastic seal-able bags she bought veg and fruit and a large bunch of lilies for Iris. On getting home she opened the medicine box in the bathroom and took out the surgical gloves putting them on carefully she went to the back of the medicine cabinet and took out a bottle of Diazepam that had belonged to her late mother.

She had always said she would return them to the chemist but never got around to it. She took six small bags and put two tablets in each then took six Tramadol out of Jeff's medicine bottle and divided them between three plastic packets that would be enough. She felt that she deserved a pat on the back for such wonderful imagination.

On the Tuesday morning Heather sat on her bench by the sycamore tree. She was lucky that the weather wasn't too warm that day and she could wear her mac nobody would get suspicious. She watched Tracy push baby Liam down the road. Sam had to be in. This would be her only chance her heart was beating like a drum as she crossed the road and climbed the stairs. The hairs on the back of her neck bristled and she could feel a slight tingling in her hands. She got to number fifteen. She rapped hard on the door and waited, she held her breath waiting for the door to open.

Sam opened the door wide what the f...

He didn't say anything else as Heather with one swift movement stuck a six inch blade into his chest. Sam made a short gurgling noise then collapsed onto the floor. Blood began to pump from his body.

Heather quickly bent and looked into his now glazed eyes

" gotcha" she whispered into his ear there was a large tear that rolled down his pale cheek. She bent down and pulled the front pockets to his jeans out, then planting a couple of bags with the pills in underneath him then another couple in his pocket. She dropped a couple of the bags just outside the door. She left the knife near the body. She removed her gloves rolling them into a ball put them into another plastic bag and put them in her pocket. She had remembered the top ten tips on Murders made easy, a web page she had found on Google.

She looked up the landing of the flats all quiet then she hurriedly flew down the staircase and onto the High street she was excited everything had gone as planned. Heather slowed down to a steady walk she didn't want to draw attention to herself. She walked through the market and called at Greggs for three vanilla slices this was a good day for every one although maybe not for Sam.

The news that evening didn't report on any incident in Bishop Horton she became agitated what if he was still alive. She was sure she had done a good job; surprisingly she was quite strong although she did look like a frail old bird. She grinned to herself, how good was that removing an evil being from the world, superwoman. By day a quiet librarian, by night a ruthless warrior. Ninja. In bed that night she listened to the local radio station but still no news. Had anyone found him, surely Tracy would have returned, the postman or another tenant she needed to sleep, work tomorrow.

Heather set off to work walking down the High Street people passed her by no eye contact with anyone she was still invisible.

Heather set up the library being first in she turned on computers and printers. Christine was the first member of staff in,

"Oh have you seen all the police at Grosvenor House flats something has gone on there's dozens of uniform officers, police cars and vans.

"Really I didn't notice anything" said Heather in her couldn't give a damn voice.

At ten o'clock that morning Jeff rang her from home it was unusual for him to ring.

"You need to come home now there is a problem, I can't speak to you over phone." Heather rang Nikki Farmer, "Nikki I need to go home Jeff has rung it's very important."

Nikki Farmer was surprised Heather never asked for time off besides her annual leave that was one thing about her she was dependable

"Of course Heather, I hope everything is alright let me know if you need more time."

"Thank you Nikki" said Heather, she knew what was going on they had found Sam.

When Heather got home there was a police car outside the house she opened the door and Claire came running towards her.

"oh mum its Sam he's dead"

"What" said Heather "I don't believe it what's happened." The police Sargent and his sidekick a young policeman who looked as though he had was just got out of school.

"I need to ask you if you have had any contact with your son in law Mrs Foster"

"Ex" corrected Heather "we don't have any contact with him and would never want it, what has happened?" Heathers face was serious.

"Yesterday Mr Grey was found at an address in the town. Unfortunately the wounds were fatal (wound corrected Heather in her head).

"Where was he found" inquired Heather, "was he at his mother's?"

"no he was found at his girlfriend's address." Claire stopped her sobbing and raised her head

"Girlfriend" she sniffed.

Heather couldn't believe her daughter after all she had been through she showed a jealous streak. The police officer asked where they all were. They would be asked to make statements at a later date at Bishop Horton police station the police would be as delicate as possible as they were aware of the situation with Mr Grey.

"Oh my god mum they think I have done it don't they"

"Don't be stupid Claire where were you yesterday?"

"At work all day we had a case conference." Sniffed Claire

"Well there you go you are in the clear."

"He had a girlfriend mum do you think he had hurt her and she stabbed him?"

"It's possible" said Heather but you don't have to worry about him anymore" she put her arms around Claire and held her as Claire sobbed not knowing why she was crying, "I have to tell the kids what am I going to say.?"

"It's going to be in the papers you don't want them to hear it at school you will have to tell them the truth."

Jeff was now watching Alaskan Gold.

"Good enough for the bastard" he said without taking his eyes from the screen, both woman had to chuckle. The papers next day reported that a man had been found with fatal stab wounds at Grosvenor House Whitehall Avenue (wound why couldn't they get it right) however the police sometimes kept things back to catch the perpetrator. She had to make sure her story was straight. The paper reported that it was a suspected drug war, the man in question had recently moved into the area, drugs had been found at the property of a twenty-two-year-old woman who was now helping police with their inquiries.

Heather knew Tracy had an alibi so she wasn't bothered about that, she only hoped she wasn't parted from baby Liam for long. That bastard using Jeff's words deserved all he got, he got his just desserts.

Jeff, Heather and Claire went to the police station the next day and were interviewed separately. Jeff had watched television all day and looked after his mother who was a bed ridden invalid. He was able to tell the officer every detail of the programmes he watched. Claire had a solid alibi as she was with nine other social workers in a case conference. Leaving work late before picking the children up from her mother's at seven o'clock.

Heathers alibi was that she was window shopping as she had annual leave so she could be home for the children when they finished school. Heather thought she should be a little vague, shopping, coffee in the High street before returning home to make tea and greet the children getting home from school.

Over the next few weeks the local newspaper ran stories relating to Sam's previous conviction and how an ex-cop had been murdered living under a pseudonym in a council flat thought to be supplying drugs to the community. Community policing thought Heather and smiled. Tracy had been released as she had been to the DSS at the time of the killing. Her neighbour Sally Briggs had found the body and rung the police. The police had thought the body had been there only about half an hour before Sally had found him.

Tracy was shocked to find that Jack was Sam and he had been in prison after abusing his wife. That was something that she wasn't shocked about. He didn't work for CSI he didn't even have a job but went to his mother's house almost every day. How could she be so stupid, she had introduced Liam to a monster it would never happen again she was not going to have another boyfriend it would be Liam and her no one else.

Sally comforted her and told Tracy that she always knew that Jack was dodgy. Who would shack up with a young mum in a council flat and live on her benefits if he had a good job it didn't make sense. Tracy thought it did make sense to her it was what she yearned for a stable home to be a family.

A couple of months had gone by. The police had called a couple of times to Heathers home just to ask questions relating to her knowledge of any of drug dealing in Sam's past. Heather was always helpful and polite although not hiding the fact that she was glad Sam was dead. The police could understand this because of his past history. The newspapers had stopped reporting the incident. It wasn't even on the back page of the newspapers no one spoke about it. Tracy was attending story time again and she looked so good there didn't seem to be a boyfriend in the background. Baby Liam was growing in to a lovely lad. Claire was happy and Mike was good for her he was still very quiet but Heather could cope with that. Work was going well although there had been problems with budgets and there was another chance that the staff would have go into consultation again it was all normal stuff.

CHAPTER TEN

Heathers spare time was now spent reading as many detective novels as possible. She read how to commit murder and how to get away with it. She scrolled the Internet for different ways to commit murder. Google surprised her at the thousands of tips on how to murder, the different poisons to use, it was all very enlightening.

As Heather lay in her cosy bed she felt very pleased with herself she had killed three people so far. She didn't feel revulsion she felt satisfaction. She had done such a good job she had helped so many people including herself of course. Mr Wilson had been a wart on society and drove her to distraction but she had played close to home especially with Sam but he had been forgotten now why would anyone want to find his murderer.

She loved this feeling of empowerment. She had heard of it before the Spice Girls even sang about it. But to feel the power through her veins was something else. She had played too close to home but Google had advised that unrelated murder was the way to go. Murder by chance was not going to happen every day so she needed to scour the town for opportunities. She had a smile upon her face as she pulled the duvet up close about her face and went to sleep.

Nikki Farmer was waiting for Heather to open the library next morning.

"Good morning Heather how are you?" she chirped

"Oh I'm fine Nikki thank you and you"
Heather was worried what disaster was about to unfold.

"I just thought I would start here today and do everyone's one to ones is that alright?"

"Of course" smiled Heather. Pity you are so close Ms Farmer you could be next but that would be stupid wouldn't it she thought.

The staff were all unnerved at their one to ones as usual. There was no threat of redundancies but Heather knew it would only be time before it shook its ugly head again. So as not to be around the office when Nikki Farmer was there Heather went out for lunch she walked down the High street and popped into Sarah's florist shop. Sarah wasn't about but she said hello to Cathy her assistant.

"Sarah's has gone to deliver a bouquet to someone in Woodside did you want me to pass a message?"

"Oh no that's fine just tell her I called. Bye."

Heather passed the Travel agents then doubled back. The posters of faraway places made her think she was due a good holiday. What was going to happen to Iris was another thing. She left the Travel agents with a large bundle of brochures all of them cruises. It seemed the best idea, Jeff could watch television all day long or go to a film. She could take part in activities on board or just laze in the sun. It would be difficult to get Jeff to go away but she could work on him and if his mother could go into a nursing home for respite care for a couple of weeks it would be wonderful.

They both settled on a Mediterranean cruise stopping in Italy. Jeff didn't really care but if it was an easy life for him he was in. They ensured Iris was happy with the nursing home for her respite care she obviously wanted a change of scenery as much as they did. June came around Heather had bought some new clothes and was so excited it was a shame Jeff had to join her. She was sure that she would have a better time without him. They joined the ship in Southampton and were both impressed with the cabin they had been expecting something similar to a cross channel ferry so it was a nice surprise. There were twin beds, a television, a lovely bathroom and a balcony, sheer luxury.

On the first evening they dressed in their formal attire Heather looked at Jeff in his tuxedo he looked a dish, why didn't he dress up at home.

"You have scrubbed up well" she said with a smile. Jeff looked in the large mirror, "yes, just call me Bond, Jeff Bond" he said with his best Sean Connery accent.

"You don't look so bad yourself I always liked you in red." That was a compliment thought Heather this could be a good holiday after all. They left the cabin hand in hand this hadn't happened for twenty years. In the dining room they were seated with two other couples and a single lady. The couples introduced themselves as Mr and Mrs Granger Bob and Angela and Mr and Mrs Walters Charles and Edith the single woman was called Corinne. Small talk went around the table and Heather chatted to the couples. Jeff was talking to Corinne who had been on numerous cruises Jeff was enthralled in her conversation. Heather sat back and took a minute to look at Miss Corinne. She was blonde about the same age as Heather maybe a couple of years younger. She was slim with very good dress sense. Heather did not like the way she laughed at Jeff's jokes Heather had raised eye brows a couple of times she had heard the jokes a hundred times and groaned inwardly.

Over the following few days Corinne turned up at the same events. Heather was cool towards her but Jeff became animated laughing joking and listening to Corinne. Heather was not happy. One night Heather took a lovely bubble bath and said she would meet Jeff in the Calypso lounge before dinner. Jeff had not stopped in the cabin as she had expected but had been part of a number of activities he was really enjoying this holiday. After spraying herself with a large dose of Clinique Happy she went to meet Jeff.

At first Heather couldn't see Jeff then she heard a shrill laugh one that she recognised, "Oh Jeff you are so funny" Corinne had her arm across Jeff's then looked up at Heather who stood smiling.

"You two look as though you are having fun' said Heather

Jeff gave that little nervous cough, "Just been waiting for you darling."

"I didn't want anyone to steal him Heather" Corinne gave a smile like the cat that had got the cream. Be careful lady thought Heather and smiled sweetly to Corinne.

"We are going to dinner Corinne are you joining us?"

"That would be lovely thank you' said Corinne a little surprised

Jeff quickly got up and the three of them went to dine. Heather and Jeff didn't see Corinne for the next couple of days it was on the last evening that they saw her after dinner in the Calypso lounge she walked up to the table.

"Hello you two have you been having a good time?" she sat next to Jeff.

Jeff coughed "lovely thank you and how has your holiday been?"

"Just lovely" she purred. They chatted a little longer then Corinne got up.

"I am going to the piano bar are you coming"

Jeff looked at Heather then said, 'No we are going to have an early night."

"Have fun then" Corinne walked away.

Heathers eyes followed her. Jeff still had a large glass of red wine in front of him Heather downed her gin, "I am going back to the cabin are coming?" she asked

"I will finish my drink first" he said. Heather left the bar and walked on to the outside deck. In front of her she could see Corinne, her long scarf with the butterflies on fluttered in the gentle breeze it was so quiet. The moon danced across the sea as Heather silently and swiftly as a bird of prey, crossed the deck.

Nine o'clock the following morning the cruise liner docked in Southampton. After breakfast Heather and Jeff disembarked in the background there was an announcement for Miss Corinne Fisher to go to the pursers' office Jeff tipped his head to hear the announcement again.

"She probably hasn't paid her bar bill" said Heather. When they arrived home Claire and the children met them at the station.

"Did you have a good time mum?" asked Claire.

"It was one of the best holidays I have ever had" Heather said with a wide smile. Claire was surprised that her father had also enjoyed himself. It was a month or two later when Jeff pointed out a small paragraph in the Daily Mail the body thought to be that of the missing cruise passenger Miss Corinne Fisher had been washed up on a beach in Brittany.

"I didn't even know she was missing did you Heather?" Heather shook her head; "I remember the ship calling her name when we were getting off".

"Oh yes I remember" said Jeff.

Heather made them both a nice cup of tea with chocolate biscuits.

CHAPTER ELEVEN

After returning to work Heather felt rested from her holiday. Things were going well. Staff were settled and Iris had a break from the humdrum of Heathers front bedroom.

Heather walked towards the market as usual and passed The Three Cups she had noticed there seemed to be a small gang of what she would call youths stood around. Since she had returned from holiday they had chosen this as their new hangout. They would stand by the benches not sit at them as normal people would. It didn't seem to matter what the weather was like they just stood or larked about swigging out of bottle necks, smoking and swearing. On this occasion they had spilled out onto the pathway and Heather had to walk into the road to avoid bumping into one lad she tutted,

"Oh your majesty I didn't see you there, ya old bag."

Heather looked at the floor as the group bayed at her as she scurried away from the throng. Bastards, you will pay didn't they know who they were dealing with.

She had made a mental note. There was seven of them three very tall guys two average height and two very short ones. One of the short ones seemed to be the leader of the pack, gobby little shit thought Heather. The short ones always had a chip on their shoulders, little man syndrome but who would have the last laugh.

Over the next few weeks Heather put up with the taunting and abuse as she tried to pass the gang. She could have taken another route but why should she. It was the easiest way home for her. There was another reason, she wanted to make the gang pay for their abuse she didn't want other people to have to suffer the same torment. She started to plan, they all had to go but if she killed all of them the police would maybe bring in the army or other police from different areas and they may have someone who would be clever. Heather could not afford to take a chance on that. Maybe one or two that would unsettle the group they may not be as cocky as they were now.

On looking through the Internet she made a list of ways to kill. She then put the list onto a saucer and set fire to it as she didn't want to leave any evidence. Maybe she could just make them very ill it could look as though they had eaten something that had upset them. Did they eat? She thought they only drank. Where they got their money from would be anybody's business. She could sell them drugs that were poisoned that might work, a bad batch they would say on True detective. Using a knife, it did give her a warm feeling and there was that act of surprise it would work well on a singular victim but not when there were so many.

Greed that was what would motivate this lot she had a plan. She went to the large supermarket on the outskirts of town and bought her weekly shopping and two large bottles of Smirnoff ice. When she unpacked them at home she hid the bottles under the bed in the small bedroom. She then read up on anti-freeze poisoning. There was a large canister of anti-freeze in the garage so she didn't have to buy it anywhere that would work well. Later that evening when Jeff was watching Alaskan off Griders she took the bottles out from the bed and poured a good quarter of the alcho pop from the two bottles she then topped up the bottles with the anti-freeze. So easy, now her only problem would be to plant it near the lads at The Three Cups it was a chance she had to take.

On leaving work Heather walked in the direction of The Three Cups. There was a small group of lads outside the pub not all of the usual ones. There were five of them, what was she going to do? The bottles clinked in the plastic bag she was carrying she held her head down. The lads were so involved in their joking about they didn't notice Heather. She slipped past and went into the pubs lobby by the front door. She left the plastic carrier. She then went to the ladies' toilet that were just inside the lobby, she waited a couple of minutes then left with her head down eyes fixed to the floor. One lad pushed another and a Staffordshire bull terrier one of the lads was holding started to bark.

"Ya wanker" cried ginger Pete.

"You're a wanker" said tattoo man, the dog jumped between the two.

Heather hurried home so not to be later than usual she didn't know if the lads would take the bait. She took the first aid gloves off and cut them into tiny pieces then put them in the bin. She just had to wait, would it work or not she had to wait and see.

"Hey Joe look at what I've just found "shouted Pete as he picked up the Tesco carrier and pulled out one of the bottles of Smirnoff ice

"Hey our lucky day." The lads laughed, Joe screwed off the cap.

"I love this stuff it's like pop" he drank almost half of the litre bottle of booze.

"leave me some you greedy bugger" Pete snatched the bottle and finished the last drop. Ben and Damian drank the other bottle between them,

"Oh poor old Zac got nothing, you snooze you lose wanker."

"And you're a greedy pair of bastards" scowled Zac "I don't like it anyways it's a tarts drink."

"Are you calling me a tart" yelled ginger Pete he held Zac by the throat.

"No Pete no" sniffled Zac

"Good job too". Pete let go of the neck of Zac and got back to drinking the pints of lager that stood on the wooden benches.

Half an hour later Joe felt his stomach, he felt ill.

"oh that lagers off "he yelled and vomited onto Zac's feet.

"Ya dirty bastard "yelled Zac.

Joe also felt bad, he had a feeling of drunkenness, the street was going around, he sat on the bench. Damien also sat down and clutched his stomach, "oh my god I feel crap too"

Ben vomited on to the road and ginger Pete laughed but too soon as he had a sharp pain in his gut.

"Bloody hell Zac go get us all a brandy that'll sort us out" Zac grudgingly went inside to the pub and bought four brandies. The group drank the alcohol and immediately felt restored, Damien and Ben said they were going home for a lie down. Ginger Pete, Joe and Zac stayed at the pub. Joe went into the pub and brought out three more brandies they threw them back, as Joe threw his head back he became unsteady on his feet, bloody hell. That had gone straight to his head the pain in his stomach twisted into a gnarling pain.

"Arggh" cried ginger Pete he couldn't focus on what was going on.

"Come on Joe lets go, give us a hand Zac".

Zac helped both lads down the street they tottered about as though they were drunk. The dog ran in and out of their feet.

"Are you pissed Zac?" asked Joe.

"I feel like it, that brandy has just pushed me over the edge." Ginger Pete had doubled over as yet another spasm of pain had snapped into his body, bloody hell.

Ginger Pete left Zac and Joe and climbed the steps to his front door he fell inside Zac could hear his mother shouting at him.

"Pissed again you bloody layabout". Mrs Shaw slapped her son at the side of his head.

"No mum I feel crap" he slurred. The dog hid behind the sofa.

"Get to bed you little sod don't be laying on this sofa I don't want sick all over take a bucket up with you." Pete took a bucket from under the sink and stumbled up to bed he flopped onto the single bed he felt like shit. He vomited again and brought his knees up to his stomach in agonising pain, Mrs Shaw turned the television up so she couldn't hear him. Pete couldn't remember what he had eaten to make him feel so ill what had he had to drink lager, brandy oh and that bottle of Smirnoff ice it could have been that. Someone must have pissed in it. He was sweating now and not sure where he was. The pain racked his body as he slowly slipped into a coma.

Next morning Mrs Shaw went into his bedroom to find Pete half out of bed he had drooled across his face and vomit filled the bed.

"You dirty drunken bastard" shouted Mrs Shaw . She got closer to her son and picked up his head it was cold she immediately dropped it and screamed then she ran down the stairs and rang the ambulance on 999. It took the ambulance only eight minutes to arrive a police car followed behind.

"I think he's dead" she said "he isn't speaking, oh it's all my fault I didn't take any notice he often comes in drunk. He was being sick everywhere so I told him to go to bed."

The ambulance man shook his head "I'm sorry he's gone"

Mrs Shaw cried. At the other side of town Damien and Ben had got to their flat each stopping to vomit along the way they laid across the settee and chairs clutching their guts.

"We need to go to the hospital" said Damien.

"No I'm not going anywhere I will be alright" Damien went into the kitchen there were dirty pans, pizza cartons, MacDonald bags, empty bean tins and dirty micro wave meal packets, gourmet dining of the teenager. Damien went to the cold water tap and put a filthy glass under it he drank two maybe three glasses before he collapsed to the floor. Damien heard the loud bang as Ben hit the floor but he couldn't do anything. Joe managed to get home although he felt disorientated he had been sick two or three times before he had got home. When he reached the front step he banged on the front door his father opened it finding his son slumped on the top step.

"what's happened Joe what is it, are you drunk what have I told you," but Joe shook his head.

"No dad no" his father looked at his son he knew this was not the usual one over the eight. Joe wasn't a bad lad and hardly ever drank too much, white foam ran down his chin.

"Dad help me"

What have you taken, is it drugs, son tell me."

"No dad I haven't"

"You must have had something"

"The Three Cups" Joe managed to slur before passing out.

Joe's father rang for an ambulance he didn't care if his son was done for drugs he needed help and quickly. The ambulance arrived on blue lights and took Joe to the same hospital that Pete would be taken to later.

After a series of tests, it was decided that Joe had ingested something but doctors were not sure what.

Damien lay in a pool of his own vomit while Ben laid in the foetal position on the sofa both unconscious. Zac knocked loudly on the door of their flat no one answered.

"Damian Ben" Zac shouted but to no avail. He lifted the letter box and could just see the outstretched body on the sofa.

"For god's sake Ben let me in." There was no sound of any other movement so Zac decided to ring the police something was not right here. The ambulance arrived and the two teenagers were taken to the local hospital," how are they?" Asked Zac.

"Not too good mate its lucky you arrived when you did". The police arrived shortly after the ambulance and they took Zac to the hospital in the patrol car.

On reaching hospital the two teenagers were taken into emergency while Zac sat in the waiting room with the police officer.

"Officer you can use this room" a nurse indicated an empty room where the police officer could interview Zac.

"Can you tell me has happened today Zac?" Zac held his head in his hands he was so confused at the situation.

"We met up at dinner time for a few drinks at The Three Cups we were just having a bit of a laugh as we do on giro day"

"Who was with you Zac?" The police officer held his pen awaiting answer.

"There was me, Ben, Damien, Ginger Pete and Joe there are usually more of us but a couple of the lads had been sanctioned so they didn't get any benefits."

"What did you have to drink at The Three Cups?"

"I had two lagers that's all, me mum takes most of my benefit money so I didn't have much to spend"

"What about the others?"

"They had had a couple more than me and they had a couple of brandies."

"Brandies that's a bit of an old man's drink isn't it?"

"Well the lads had found some Smirnoff ice on the bench so they drank that between them, I didn't have any. About half an hour after that they started to get sick. Oh my god what about Joe and Pete" the lad looked truly concerned as to his friend's demeanour. The officer said he would check to see if they had been taken to hospital. Zac settled down in the waiting room he had tried Joe and Pete on his mobile but there was no answer he was worried.

PC Palmer asked the receptionist about the other friends. They had a Joe Webster who was deceased on arrival at the hospital then there was a Peter Shaw who was critical in ICU. There was no information yet on the two new cases. Hours later a doctor stood in front of PC Palmer and Zac.

Zac knew it was bad news before the doctor opened his mouth.

"I am sorry but both young men have died, do you know if they have any family? The doctor seemed embarrassed as he asked the question.

"No they haven't" said Zac "they came out of the children's home with me," he started to cry the PC put his arm awkwardly around the tough looking kid who had now reverted to being a small child that needed a hug.

Pete's dad watched his son behind a glass screen. His son had a number of tubes coming out of his body but he was still alive. Not so his mates Damien, Ben and Joe. Pete's dad thought they had been taking some sort of drug. Kids these days tried all sorts of stuff he had heard of legal highs stuff made from fertilizer and rat droppings why are kids so stupid. He couldn't leave Pete he was his only child his wife had died when Pete was only two and he had brought him up alone. It had been tough and Pete had gone off the rails a bit but he wasn't a bad lad.

The doctor approached Mr Webster "Good morning sir I am afraid it has been a long night and Pete is not out of the woods yet, do you have ethylene glycol at home?"

"I don't have any chemicals at home doctor" Mr Webster felt affronted.

"Ethylene Glycol is usually found in ant-freeze."

"Well yes I have a container of that in the garage I get a new one every year, is that what he has taken? The bloody little fool."

"It is what we think it may be we will not be sure until later today. The police officer will go to your home and pick the container up and any other that contains it, do you have any de-icer in your car or under the sink,"

Mr Webster thought for a moment "yes I think I have".

Heather wandered from work down the High street she noticed that outside The Three Cups there was just one lad nursing a pint of lager she joyfully skipped passed and onto home. There wasn't anything in the newspapers that day or the day after. She wondered if her lethal cocktail had worked. The following day the headlines said it all, Three Young Men Die in Poisoning the report explained that the men and died by ingesting ethylene glycol, it was thought that it was a deliberate act and the substance was added to a drink that was found outside of The Three Cups public house. Another young man was in intensive care. Police are asking for any witnesses who were in the area on Tuesday afternoon. Police also said that any information would be treated as confidential.

Heather was ecstatic three out of five how good was that. The greedy little sods they just couldn't help themselves. Pity about the last one but there must be a chance of him dying. She didn't want him to live and be disabled as she knew it could cause blindness she didn't want him to be in pain or be a burden on his family. What a bonus it reads as though the police think it could be gang related.

Zac was allowed to visit his friend he watched through the glass of the ICU what the hell how did it get to here. A couple of days ago they were acting the fool outside The Three Cups larking about, now three of his friends were dead and one as good as dead. From now on he had to make his time precious he didn't want to be left like this he decided there and then not to drink again and not waste his life as he had been doing.

The police first thought it was a gang related problem there were a number of gangs in the area although nothing on the scale of London or Bristol. The injuries then were usually stabbings or drive by shootings. This was a little more sophisticated for gang warfare. It was now established that at lunchtime or early afternoon someone had left two bottles of Alcho pop outside The Three Cups both bottles had been doctored with Ethylene Glycol probably anti-freeze from someone's garage. The ethylene glycol was sweet tasting so the lads would not taste anything different. The police found the bottles but only the fingerprints of the lads were found. There wasn't anything different about the bottles it was a very popular drink it had been bought at the large Tesco supermarket outside Mapplebeck and Police were looking at CCTV footage.

Heather walked up the High street she was so happy she felt as though she had won the lottery. It was such a good feeling, empowerment. She had not felt like that for such a long time. Her grown up children didn't make her feel empowered anymore the only time she was needed by them was when she had to babysit or someone to borrow money from. Jeff, my god Jeff, the only thing that he needed from her was to ensure his meals were in front of him three times a day and his clothes were washed and ironed. She was full time carer to his mother while he watched Off Grid Alaska. She had become Jeff's mother in fact she had become everyone's mother.

She needed something in her life something to give her that buzz that she had had when she was seventeen before she had met Jeff when she was master/mistress of her own life. Enjoying the freedom only the young can experience. Not being frightened of doing anything or saying something. Not upsetting anyone, to breathe fresh air to be Hev not Heather. Things seemed crystal clear nothing mugged her brain she enjoyed what she was doing. Clearing the detritus off the face of the earth. The police couldn't do it anymore they were restricted by laws, they had so much paperwork these days. She was The Equalizer taking back the streets from the bad and evil.

"I am scared" said Christine this mad man could strike anywhere; we need to put some security in place here Heather"

"We don't have alcohol on the premises Christine" Heather pointed out as she opened the front doors to the Library.

"No but this stuff can be added to anything because it tastes sweet they can put it in your tea."

"Well we will only drink coffee from now on" smiled Heather.

"You know what I mean" said Christine a little deflated at the way Heather dismissed her idea. Heather thought she would cheerfully add it to Christine's tea just for a little peace and quiet.

"I think we are quite security conscious Christine, if anything is found about the library we are not going to drink it we are all adults."

"Yes I suppose so" Christine was not quite sure she would pour away a bottle of alcohol without trying it first.

Heather loved reading the local newspapers there were so many stories about the poisoning's. She had surprised herself that she felt sorry for the father of one of the boys the one that was still alive. The lad was blind and deaf so he was still a burden on society. The stories were amazing where did the reporters get their stories from, it was hoped that the police never read them or there would never be any arrests. Police were following a line of enquiry and that CCTV footage was being scrolled through at supermarkets and shops in the district. I won't hold my breath then thought Heather.

CHAPTER TWELVE

Claire, Mike and the children arrived at Heathers house at twelve- thirty on Sunday. The children had their IPads already with ear phones sticking out of their Beany hats. Claire was beaming and stood in the kitchen with Heather.

"Can I do anything to help?" Heather immediately raised her head, somethings up? Claire s hands rested on the counter top and Heather saw on Claire's left hand a large diamond solitaire.

"He has popped the question then, has he been to ask your dad for permission?"

"Don't be daft mum nobody does that these days anyways this is the second time, hopefully second time lucky."

Let's hope so thought Heather.

"Go show your dad then", Claire bounded into the lounge holding her hand out in front of her. Jeff managed to squint at the ring just as Robson Green caught his tackle on some bushes.

"No sense you young'uns."

"Dad don't be like that".

The children sang here comes the bride forty inches wide. "Stop it children" said Heather. Mike sat on the sofa never uttering a word but blushed from his socks to his ears

"Are you getting married or just staying engaged" said Heather trying to sound interested.

"Married of course" said Claire "We don't want to be living in sin. We thought we would have a nice quiet wedding next June, after everything that's happened it would be better that way."

Heather nodded, "Yes sensible" she hoped she didn't want her and Jeff to fork out any more money. It was enough the last time, what was it fifteen thousand pounds or near enough. Sam's mother was a widow so couldn't contribute much. Heather thought she may have paid for the flowers but that was all. What you do for your children and they hardly ever speak to you without wanting something at the end of it.

"Mike is going to pay for everything so you don't have to worry "said Claire "he is so generous but if you would like to make a donation towards the honeymoon we would be grateful."

"Honeymoon, anywhere nice?"

"Yes Mauritius it's in the Indian ocean"

"Yes I know" answered Heather

Charlie perked up, "Are we going?"

"No Charlie it's a honeymoon children don't really go on honeymoon with their parents."

"Well what about us?" Yes, what about you thought Heather.

"I am sure your Grandma and Granddad would love to have you for two whole weeks, wouldn't you mum? They would still be at school because its late June so you wouldn't have to have any time off work."

"Alright Claire give me the dates when you have booked,"

"I have booked already, we get married on the tenth and fly out on the eleventh flying back on the twenty fifth. All-inclusive mum so I don't have to do anything just be waited on hand and foot. Nothing unusual about that, thought Heather as she laid the dining table.

Claire never stopped talking throughout the meal the children still had their earphones in and Mike just nibbled at his food. Mike was going to move in to her house because it was in a better area than Mikes but they were going to buy new furniture together that would make it a home for both of them a new start.

"I thought you would be pleased mum you never say anything; you lead such a mundane life I thought this would perk you up a bit you are pleased for me?"

"Of course I am Claire I'm just a bit tired that's all and I don't have a mundane life there's always something happening."

"What in the library" scoffed Claire, "who stole the chocolate biscuit brigade." Heather didn't like Claire when she tried to be superior, after all the things that she had sorted out in Claire's life my goodness if she only knew half of it.

Heather watched Jeff eat his Sunday lunch he didn't say much either he was probably wondering how much it would cost him, this honeymoon. At six thirty the children complete with ear phones, Mike and Claire wafted out of the family home leaving Heather and Jeff to mull over the afternoons event.

"How much is that going to bloody cost, then how much, we can't afford another wedding you had better tell her, no fancy stringed quartet, releasing doves and butterflies like the last one.

No chance, we need to conserve our money you don't know if your jobs safe yet and I will never get another one not at my age and my back".

Wow thought Heather that must have been his longest speech for a decade that's stirred the bugger up.

CHAPTER THIRTEEN

It was getting close to Christmas and the market place seemed very festive with a large Christmas tree sent by the twin town in Norway. It was lit by hundreds of multi coloured bulbs. Every evening at 6.15pm St Patrick's choir sang Christmas Carols to the work tired people of Bishop Horton. Heather loved the whole spectacle of the tree and the pretend snow on its branches to the choir boys dressed in their red cassocks and battery lit candles. There was a man selling hot chestnuts and all the High Street shops had dressed their windows. There was a very Dickensian atmosphere you only needed Bob Cratchit walking down the road with Tiny Tim on his shoulder and you had it all.

She passed The Three Cups but there was only a solitary smoker on the wooden benches outside but she could see inside the pub. There was a fake log fire burning brightly and a number of people standing around the bar. She wondered if any of the lad's parents were in there thinking of their dear departed sons. She had to admit that things were very quiet at the moment she needed a project but she wasn't thinking of knitting a jumper.

Over the past months she had been researching different poisons, it was a woman's tool she thought. Men tended to go for a more brutal approach although she had experienced that herself and she did get a lot of pleasure out of the action.

The police had never come up with any names or reason why Sam had been murdered the general idea was that Sam had tried to cash in on drugs in the area, a new boy so to speak and the local drug baron didn't like someone on their turf so they murdered him. Sounded perfectly reasonable to her. She did have to think and smile to herself as she remembered Sam's last look and the surprise in his eyes.

The police had been in contact with Claire Jeff and herself to bring them up to speed the police man said. She often wondered what that phrase meant. What it did mean was that the police didn't have a bloody clue. There was a picture in the local news of one of the Fathers with his wheelchair bound disabled son. His dad stood gauntly at his side it was the first Christmas without his friends and they wanted all the people of Bishop Horton to remember the devastating loss they had experienced and the news that the police were no further in apprehending the culprit or culprits.

Heather had offered to help out at the soup kitchen over the Christmas week. Well everyone had to help out those that couldn't help themselves. Heather watched the vagrants that had gathered for the free food. She ladled hot tomato soup into polystyrene cups. She could have used some of her magic formula here it would save the tax payer a bob or two but it was too close to home she couldn't afford to get sloppy and this lot looked so pathetic.

She handed an old woman who was wearing a man's grey overcoat a slice of very dry white sliced bread.

"Thank you love if it wasn't for people like you I don't know where we would be." The old woman chirped.

She took a slurp of the soup and grinned a toothy grin with a now red moustache on her upper lip.

"Your welcome sweetheart, here get some more bread" the old woman took the bread then stared hard at Heather.

"I know you don't I? I've seen you before."

"Have you" smiled Heather, "I work on the High street in the library."

"No, no, it's not there," the old woman squinted at Heather again then walked away but looked back a couple of times as though to draw a face from her memory.

The soup cauldron was taken away and a huge plateful of mince pies was handed around then cups of tea. Heather went towards the old woman with the plate of pies, "Here we are my love, a nice mince pie and a cup of tea" the old woman took two pies but no tea.

"I know where I have seen you before, you live in Grosvenor House don't you I go down there sometimes to get left over sandwiches at the take away, it is you" said the old woman spitting crumbs of mince pie out and feeling satisfied she had remembered.

"No sorry you are mistaken" said Heather "you must have mixed me up with someone else." Heather could feel the warmth rising to her cheeks.

"No I never forget a face, I did, I did see you." The old woman pointed at her.

Heather smiled and walked away, shit someone had seen her she hadn't banked on that but who would believe an old tramp, she had to think quickly. The old woman ate her pies and then folded up what looked like an old blanket put it into a shopping trolley and waved bye to everyone. She was muttering to herself as she pushed the trolley down the High street through the market place and onto the tow path under the arches of the bridge over the canal. It was an ideal place to bed down you were never disturbed there you could get out of the wind too and she had a full belly tonight that didn't happen very often. She thought of that woman at the soup kitchen. She had remembered her why didn't she want to say where she lived. Grosvenor House flats were lovely and the park opposite was nice and clean. She had seen that woman coming out of the flats and she had seen her once before sitting in the gardens near the big sycamore tree. Now that was strange.

Heather had that dreaded feeling when Gracie had said she had seen her at Grosvenor House she thought that when she became invisible she was invisible to everyone but that didn't seem to be the case. What had she to do, well there was a simple solution. She didn't acknowledge Gracie knowing her, she just smiled and nodded but she could feel the stare of the old woman burning into her back as she walked away.

The pots and pans were cleared away and the clients as they were called by the group got their belongings together and wandered away looking for a bed for the night. Heather said her goodbyes to everyone then stood to one side. Gracie was walking down the High street mumbling to herself. Heather started to walk that way but kept stopping and looking in shop windows, Gracie walked through the market place and towards the tow path, Heather didn't go through the market place she went to the front of The Three Cups not many people about but she had a little coughing fit a couple smoking outside saw her but didn't offer any help but they did see her she was sure. It would be a useful alibi if she needed one.

On the other side of the pub Heather ran down the snicket to the tow path she saw Gracie in front.

Heather looked around for a weapon she saw half a brick the old woman was still muttering to herself and singing

There is an orphanage just beyond the park
There in the big top room there is many a lark
Oh you should see them run when they hear the
matron come
Six strikes across their bums all in the dark

She gave a little laugh then a groan as Heather smashed the brick into the back of the old woman's skull. Gracie didn't think another thought, there was a loud explosion in her head then she thought no more.

As Gracie fell to the floor Heather kicked the starved body into the canal it hardly made a splash she then carried the brick further along the tow path and deposited it gently into the canal. Heather had to be quick she walked over the bridge and home.

"Is that you" cried Jeff

Who the hell do you think it would be thought Heather "No its the bogey man" she shrilled still trying to catch her breath.

"Silly bugger" said Jeff.

Heather laid in bed she felt satisfied with the evenings event helping the poor unfortunates of the world some more unfortunate than others. It had made her think though; she had thought she was completely invisible but that old woman had seen her she had remembered her from Grosvenor House how strange she couldn't remember seeing the old woman.

Next morning Heather stood for five minutes in front of the hall mirror she couldn't see what the old woman had seen there was a slight puff of white hair and her cheeks did have a little colour but that was it.

Heather walked down the High street looking at people directly in the face to try and catch a glimpse of recognition, nothing, people were hurriedly dodging around her no one ever looked at her, they were looking immediately ahead or at the floor there was no eye contact. She reached the library to find Christine and Pam waiting for her.

"Heather have you heard they have found another body in the canal."

"Another" said Heather "when did they find the last one?"

"No what I meant to say a body murdered like the one at Grosvenor House" said Christine.

"They were stabbed?" asked Heather.

"Yes, no, someone had chucked the old girl into the canal, poor old woman never hurt anyone in her whole life then whack, someone takes a dislike to you, your face doesn't fit then wham Bam thank you mam"

"Give up Christine you are a proper doom merchant" said Pam

Christine was quite put out by Pam's remark Pam very rarely said anything or past comment maybe she was having a bad day.

"Come on let's get this show on the road." Said Heather

Christine asked if she could nip out for a minute and came back with vanillas for everyone just to say sorry for earlier.

On Sunday morning Heather got up and prepared things for the lunch. Claire Mike and the kids would be around as usual about one. At ten thirty the doorbell rang and Heather went to the front door on opening it she found two policemen one carrying a clip board, "Good morning is it Mrs Foster?"

"Yes can I help you officers, please come in" she showed the police officers into the lounge Jeff almost fell out of his chair," bloody hell what's up now?"

"Sorry to startle you sir, we have come to see your wife"

"What's she been up to then?" questioned Jeff

"Jeff be quiet let the officer speak"

"Thank you, we are making inquiries as to the death of a Mrs Grace Kitchen did you know her?"

"No" said Heather "I don't think I do."

"I understand you had worked at the soup kitchen this weekend." Asked the tall officer.

"Yes I did a shift on Friday I always help out at Christmas, oh no Grace you mean Gracie I am sorry I didn't know her full name she isn't the person found in the canal is she? Oh no" Heather sat on the edge of the sofa.

"Poor Gracie yes I actually spoke to her she had a couple of my mince pies the poor old dear did she fall into the canal."

"We don't know just what happened but we do believe it was a little more than an accident"

"The poor woman, she never hurt a fly there are some evil people about officer it makes me feel a bit frightened why would anyone do such a thing. It isn't as though she was wealthy she hadn't two farthings to rub together. She didn't know where her next meal was coming from." Heather thought she might try out for the local Amateur Dramatic society in the New Year.

The officer asked at what time she left the soup kitchen, what was the route she had taken home and the time she got in.

"If there is anything you need to ask me please don't hesitate, I work at the library so you know where I am if you need me". Heather could tell that the police officer who was asking the questions wasn't really listening to her, he was writing her answers but he was watching Robson Green land a giant Marlin, boy just look at that magnificent creature"

"They sure are" said Jeff "that's what I would like to do when I'm retired,"

Charming thought Heather, you retired five years ago. The police men thanked her and left.

CHAPTER FOURTEEN

Next day Heather stood at the desk situated in the centre of the library she was sorting through index cards; they were always in a mess after Christine had finished with them. Heather was sure that Christine didn't know her alphabet.

"Hello Heather" a soft voice spoke her name Heather raised her eyes to be met by a very short woman with violet eyes she wore a faux fur coat and a knitted hat over steely grey hair. For a moment Heather wasn't sure who she was then click.

"Hello Maggie how are you?" She didn't smile at the woman as she pricked Heathers conscience just a little but only for a passing moment.

"I'm fine Heather" the woman smiled.

"what can I do for you" questioned Heather she didn't want to spend any more time on this person than was necessary.

"I will come straight to the point as I can see you are very busy."

"Yes I am."

"Well it's difficult isn't it"

"Yes" snapped Heather.

"Heather I want to see the children. I haven't seen them since Sam was arrested I love them they are my grandchildren as well as yours." Her voice had risen and Christine had put her head around the stock room door.

"Are you alright Heather?"

94

"Yes thank you" said Heather glaring at Christine.

"Please Heather, Claire won't take my calls I am not sure if it's the right number. Heather I am ill, very ill and I want to meet up with the children."

Heather thought she didn't look ill she looked the same as the last time she had seen her at the Crown Court supporting her abusive dead beat son.

"I can't tell Claire what to do Maggie, she has her own mind now she is happy the kids are happy and for your information she has a lovely fiancée who treats her well not as a punch bag."

"Please Heather" Maggie stood with tears running down her face.

"I am sure you could help me, Claire listens to you." Heather raised her eyes like hell she thought. However, Maggie's pleading had struck a chord, yes she still did have a heart.

"Alright Maggie I will speak to her I don't think she would want to meet you but I will try to be a mediator."

"Thank you Heather thank you" she dabbed her eyes with a tissue, "this is my new number I don't have a fixed line now just a mobile number. I will meet anywhere or they can come to me."

Heather took the paper with the number scribbled on it.

"I will speak to you soon" Heather dismissed her, Maggie nodded and scuttled from the library resembling a moth eaten bear.

Christine came from the stockroom, "Who was that?"

"Claire's ex mother in law" said Heather gathering a pile of books.

"Oh my god how could she, she's a bit brazen isn't she?"

Heather didn't answer she didn't talk about family with staff the more they know the more they wanted to know. When Heather got home that night she rang Claire," Hi love I had a visitor at the library today," Claire could tell by Heathers voice it was serious "Who" she asked there was a pause, "Sam's mother Maggie"

"Oh gawd will I never be free from that man" she shrieked.

"Claire she is their grandmother and she says she is very ill."

"Well I don't care" announced Claire, "they are not seeing her. She will want to tell them all lies about her precious son. Not about what he did to me or them for that matter she won't be telling them about his drug dealing and abuse and his grisly end, I don't want that mum."

"I don't think she would do that Claire she just wants to see them. They had a relationship with her she wasn't the monster, she was their Grannie why don't you ask them.

"If they want to see her. No" Claire slammed down the phone.

Well I expected that thought Heather. Half an hour later Claire rang back,

"I am not meeting her mum I don't trust her after all this time it's a scandal."

"Calm down Claire it will be alright children are resilient I can take them for a visit, we can meet in a cafe in town it will be easier."

"Alright next weekend I spoke to the kids and they wanted to see her."

"I will ring and organize it, I will ring you back with the details."

Heather took the card from her bag and rang the mobile number.

"Hello Maggie its Heather"

"Yes" there was a glimmer of hope in Maggie's voice.

"Will next weekend be ok, Sunday morning I can meet you in the Park cafe at eleven thirty is that alright?"

"OK oh thank you Heather I will never be able to thank you enough"

"Maggie there is one thing, you mustn't speak about Sam. The kids have gone through enough and this is not the time to go into details you can answer any questions the children have but we don't want to bring up the past."

"I agree to anything I just want to see the children."

"Well next Sunday eleven thirty for an hour."

"That's fine thank you Heather.

The following Sunday soon came and Claire arrived with the children, "Just watch her mum I told you I don't trust her". At eleven o'clock Heather put on her coat, "Come on kids lets have you." The kids seemed quite eager to go and chatted easily with Heather on the way to the park.

When they arrived at the cafe they found a table near to the window Heather bought cans of coke for the kids and a cup of coffee for herself. The cafe was almost full as it was a sunny winters day.

"It's Grannie" shouted Charlie who jumped out of her seat, Luke followed "Yeh Grannie."

They ran from the cafe and into the arms of Maggie the group were crying and laughing all at the same time. Heather was astonished she didn't realize the children had such a good relationship with their other grandmother. The happy throng entered the cafe Maggie's face was bright and wet with tears.

"Thank you Heather you don't know what this means to me."

"You are welcome" said Heather but deep in the pit of her stomach she felt sick with jealousy by the way the children made such a fuss of Maggie. The children never took their eyes off the beaming face of their other grandmother.

Maggie had bought two presents wrapped up in bright paper. Charlie ripped the paper with glee.

"What is it, what is it?" she chirped. It was a beautiful glass jewellery box painted with butterflies, when the box was opened a tiny ballerina twirled to the plonkity plonk song of Whitney Houston's 'I will always love you'.

"Oh its beautiful Grannie I love it" she gave Maggie a big hug and a kiss. Luke shouted, "Now me, now me," he was so excited he ripped the paper from the gift. It was a money box in the shape of Dr Who's Tardis. He rattled it and was pleased to hear the sound of numerous coins.

"Wow Grannie its brilliant it's the best present ever."

Kids, thought Heather fickle, her stomach was churning as the jealousy ate into her colon giving her gripey pains she almost vomited.

"Calm down you two" chastised Heather. The children chatted away as they ate their Penguin biscuits they would now and again cuddle up to Maggie who warmly encased her arms around them. Heather hated her there and then they hadn't seen or heard from this woman for what, nearly two years and in she comes, no by your leave buying her grandchildren gifts how bloody dare she.

"It's time to go children" both children grumbled.

"Thank you Heather I can never thank you enough you don't know what this means to me."

"That's OK Maggie" Heather said through gritted teeth.

"Can I see them again?" asked Maggie with an eagerness in her voice. Heather knew this would happen.

"I will have to ask Claire it isn't up to me."

"Yes I understand" said Maggie "I will wait to hear from you then."

Heather gathered the wrapping paper up and gave it to the girl behind the counter. The children gave their Grannie a hug and said they wanted to meet up again. Heather said they would have to ask their mother. Good byes said and done the children walked in front of Heather, the kids looked happy they didn't show that much enthusiasm with her or Jeff, what a bitch.

Claire was waiting at home she had done the veg for lunch which was a bonus for Heather. The kids were still excited and showed their gifts to their granddad and mother. They ran up the stairs to show their presents to their great Grannie. "How dare she" said Claire "after all this time" Heather nodded in agreement.

"They are not going again mum" this statement was interrupted by Charlie who announced that she wanted to meet her Grannie next week.

"I don't think that's possible" said Claire looking at her mother for moral support. "We shall have to wait and see" said Heather.

"Aw it's not fair" wailed Charlie.

"Stop it Charlie' cautioned Claire. Charlie stamped her foot and went into the lounge. "Look what's happened already that bloody woman" Claire was furious. Yes, thought Heather that bloody woman. On Monday morning Heather had a visitor.

"There is someone to see you Heather she said she is a family member' said Pam. Heather walked on to the library floor Maggie was smiling at her, bloody family member what the hell ,how dare she the cheek.

"Hello Heather' said Maggie with a broad smile Heather noticed the dark circles around her eyes maybe she was ill.

"What are you doing here'? said Heather a little rudely.

"OH I am sorry to call at your work but I had to say thank you again for yesterday" Heather tried to remain calm "No problem Maggie, after all you are their Grannie it was good to see them so happy."

The bare faced cheek of this woman thought Heather rubbing it in with the kids.

"It's almost lunchtime, how about we go for a sandwich?"

"Oh no I don't think so' said Heather.

"Oh please Heather I would love to have a chat with you." Heather agreed and they met at the Blue Bird cafe just on the High street. Heather ordered a ham and tomato sandwich, Maggie a tuna mayo they both had steaming mugs of latte.

"This is such a treat' said Maggie.

"Yes' answered Heather not really caring.

Heather changed the subject from food, "you said you were very ill Maggie can I ask what the trouble is. Is there anything we can do for you?' she knew she had to change her tactics.

"You can't do anything I'm afraid I'm beyond help so to speak, oh dear that sounds daunting. I have brain cancer I have had some treatment but it hasn't helped. Nothing seems to have improved things. The cancer has now gone to my lymph glands so you see I had to make contact with the children again before I go.'

"I can understand that' said Heather.

"I don't think I have much time Heather so I want to spend as much time as possible with my grandchildren. You are so understanding Heather.' Maggie touched Heathers hand, Heather felt her skin creep she slowly drew her hand away.

"I have so much to say to them' said Maggie not noticing Heathers distance towards her.

"What you need to do Maggie is to write them a letter each and maybe one to Claire to tell them how you feel' suggested Heather.

"Heather, you are right I will do that and when I die the letters could be passed to them' Maggie had a sparkle in her eyes, "I will get onto it straight away.'

"It's such a good way of passing things on' said Heather "you can't always say things face to face, do you want me to keep the letters Maggie I am happy to do that.'

"You are so kind Heather' Maggie clutched Heathers hand again.

"No worries I am just pleased that I can help it's such a sad situation' Heather allowed Maggie's hand to rest for a moment.

They agreed that Heather would call after work on Thursday. She would do a bit of shopping at the big Tesco's then call at Maggie's house in Mapplebeck

When Heather got home she searched the back of the medicine cabinet for the Diazepam and Tamazapan tablets that she had kept from her mother's medicine cabinet. She wasn't sure how many she would need so she Googled it. Very interesting she may even be able to change career and go into pharmacy. Maggie may not need much if she was taking other drugs. Heather was equipped with her pills, a pair of plastic gloves from the first aid kit. This aside it all depended on the letters would Maggie have written them.

Heather did a small shop on Thursday so she didn't have to carry much she went to Maggie's house in Mapplebeck. Heather remembered the house as she had been there on a few family occasions when Claire and Sam were married.

"Heather please come in its lovely to see you, come in, come in.' Heather was ushered into the lounge I will make us a pot of tea, make yourself comfortable'

Heather looked around the cramped lounge there was a couple of photographs of Sam on the wall and two silver frames with the smiling faces of her grandchildren on their first day at school. Heathers eyes were then drawn to the three large white envelopes on the shelf above the fireplace. The top one read Charlie, yes she had written them the excitement grew in Heathers body, there was a tingling in her toes.

Maggie came into the lounge carrying a tray with two cups and saucers a milk jug sugar bowl and teapot she placed it on the small table in front of them.

"Maggie could I beg you for a biscuit please I need to take a pill and it has to be with food nothing dreadful just old age and poverty.'

"Of course, I will be a minute I should have brought biscuits in anyways I am so rude.'

Maggie disappeared into the kitchen, Heather opened her bag and took out the small plastic bag of crushed tablets she emptied them into Maggie's cup she then poured hot tea onto them stirring to dissolve them as much as possible she added milk stirring again. Maggie opened the door, "I'm being mother, sugar? Heather asked.

"Two please I have a sweet tooth." Heather piled the sugar onto the spoon twice and stirred the tea again. Maggie took the cup and saucer and sipped the hot tea.

"Heather I didn't think that you would ever speak to me again but I should have known, you are a mother and you are a grandmother, I should have known.' Maggie took another sip of her tea she placed the cup in the saucer and added another spoonful of sugar, "I shouldn't but what the hell.' Maggie drank more tea then topped it up from the pot.

"Am I alright to go to the loo Maggie'

"Of course you are, it's still in the same place, top of the stairs first on the right." Heather went into the bathroom carefully trying not to touch anything she put on the plastic gloves she had in her pocket she opened the medicine cabinet it was crammed full of pills. Heather had heard of some of them but not all, there was also some small phials of a clear substance she thought she may need it so put half a dozen in her pocket.

Returning to the lounge Maggie was slumped in the chair,

"I am sorry Heather I feel a bit strange."

"Let me help you I will pour you another drink" said Heather picking the teapot up.

"No a glass of water, water" she slurred. Heather went to the kitchen and took a glass that was on the draining board she poured the contents of two of the phials into the glass and ran water into it.

"Here we are Maggie" she helped Maggie with the glass, Maggie stared blankly at Heather.

"More please water" Heather took the glass and went to the kitchen again depositing a couple more phials of the drug, Maggie tipped the glass to her lips she laughed, "Heather you have monkey hands" Maggie lost consciousness. Heather looked at her gloved hands yes the plastic gloves did make them look like a monkey's hand.

Heather opened two more phials of the drug and poured it down Maggie's throat she then placed the tiny plastic phials onto the saucer of Maggie's cup she went into the kitchen and washed her own cup saucer and teaspoon and put them in their rightful place she put the chocolate biscuits into her coat pocket.

Heather took the three letters from the mantel piece and placed them on the tray propped up by the teapot Heather looked around the room and the scene set before her, no one would know Maggie had a visitor. She waited half an hour then took the makeup mirror from her handbag and placed it by Maggie's mouth there was no breath. Maggie had a little drizzle of white foam at the corner of her mouth, Heather didn't touch it. Heather dropped the latch and quietly closed the front door and went home. Lamb chops and new potatoes for tea.

On Saturday Claire arrived at the library in a bit of a state, "mum I need to speak to you."

"What's wrong love?"

They went into the library stock room, Pam was putting books onto a trolley when she saw Claire and Heather, Pam left discreetly. Claire was sobbing, Pam thought what on earth has happened to that family again.

"Oh mum that bloody woman." Sniffed Claire.

"What's happened?"

"Mum its Maggie she has committed suicide. Her Macmillan nurse called yesterday at the house and was worried she didn't answer the door, she had taken loads of pills, what am I going to tell the kids they have gone through enough."

"To top it all she had written letters to me and the kids. Mum will I never be rid of that family?" Claire cried onto her mother's clean white blouse.

"She was ill Claire." Consoled Heather.

"But why did she have to get in touch with the children, why drag them into this pantomime it's not fair."

"The police again at my house, the neighbours will think I am a mass murderer."

"No they won't" said Heather, "it will be another seven-day wonder, come on at least she's out of our lives for good,"

"Mum" Claire hugged her mother.

Heather smiled at her daughter, "We have a wedding to plan" Claire smiled and went back to her new fiancé and children feeling so much better.

In the afternoon Christine stood close to Heather at the library desk, "I'm so sorry to hear about Claire's mother in law'

"Ex mother in law" corrected Heather, "Where did you hear that Christine'

"I know Mrs Grey's MacMillan nurse Vanessa, she knows I can keep a secret working for the council."

Heather raised her eyebrows, "I don't want to hear anything else Chris please". Christine moved away a little hurt that Heather had reprimanded her.

Nikki Farmer found Heather in the stock room, "Hello Heather are you ok? Christine has told me about your bad news" Bloody hell couldn't she have any privacy.

"Do you want to go home early I am sure the others can manage." Nikki Farmer exercised her authority.

"No I am fine thank you" said Heather.

"But I insist" said Nikki "I have a duty of care."

As Heather took her coat and walked across the library floor she caught the eye of Christine who stood by the criminal fiction her eyes met hers Christine looked away quickly, she felt the touch of death.

Heather was furious she had been sent home but what could you do when your manager insists. Jeff didn't ask why she was home early he just heard the kettle go on and shouted, "I will have one." Heather took his tea in on a tray complete with chocolate biscuits, "wow we are coming up in the world" and took a handful of biscuits.

"Sam's mother has committed suicide Jeff; Claire has been to the library this morning."

"Bloody hell did she seem like that type when you took the kids to see her."

"No" whatever that type was, "she was just happy to see them." Jeff grunted the conversation was over.

As Heather laid in her bed that night. She was pleased with herself, it was a shame that Maggie couldn't live her last few months in the bosom of her family. Heather thought it had been a blessing no hospitals, hospices no piles of drugs, she had done the best thing it was definitely a blessing.

CHAPTER FIFTEEN

On Thursday it was story time. Tracy joined the group with baby Liam. She looked so much more mature now, her hair had been cut into a neat bob. She didn't look gaunt and baby Liam was now toddling about joining in with the story. "Once upon a time" "Once upon a time" he would repeat At the end of story time the women pushed their chairs back making a nerve cringing screech the toys were replaced into the relevant boxes. Heather gathered the books to return to the shelf.

"Heather" a quiet voice spoke, Heather turned around it was Tracy.

"I just want to say thank you for all you have done for me and Liam."

"I haven't done anything Tracy" smiled Heather.

"Yes you have, you have never questioned me you have just been there, thank you."

"Are you doing OK Tracy?"

"Yes, after the New Year I am doing a college course, I think I want to go into nursing"

"That's wonderful, go out there and show everyone" Tracy smiled and pushed Liam's buggy into the High Street.

Heather felt elated all that messing about resulted in success all around.

Christmas came and went with its usual surprises and disappointment's. Heather got her usual pair of slippers from Claire, a box of toiletries from Tom and Sarah and a pair of silk like pyjamas still in the Aldi plastic bag from Jeff saying he hadn't time to wrap them properly. They were also two sizes too small, he was so dependable.

For New Year's Eve Heather, Jeff, Claire, Mike and the kids with Iris dressed in her party frock went to Tom and Sarah's house.

"Come in Come in" welcomed Tom. The house was decorated so beautifully with wreaths hung on the doors and gold and silver baubles in large glass vases. Sarah glided through the room in a stylish outfit ensuring the cushions were plumped up on the sofa.

Tom stood by the fireplace he was so handsome. Tall, broad shouldered with a friendly manner everyone was Toms friend. Her father had the same manner he was always life and soul of the party but Tom was alive and vital her father was buried in the dark earth.

CHAPTER SIXTEEN

Heather looked at her father in the bed in the back bed room. It wasn't the ideal place for him to be but how could she not have her own father when she was already looking after her mother in law. Her father and mother had been divorced for a number of years. Her father depended on her for the weekly shopping, trips to the doctors, hospital etc. etc. He had been injured during the war and had numerous ailments and mental health issues. Thomas had recently had to undergo surgery for a brain haemorrhage. This had been successful but he had been told not to drink. This did not go down too well with Thomas and as soon as he was able he was at the pub. He liked living with Heather he would go to the pub on a lunch time. Heather would have tea for him when he got in, he didn't have to hand over all his pension as he had when he was married. He also liked the fact that Heather felt duty bound, as she had Iris living in the house already. Jeff liked a drink in the evening just as he did and they got on well enough.

For Heather it was a nightmare, her father was drunk everyday he took handfuls of pills some she didn't have any idea what they were for but she was sure he shouldn't be taking what he did. The pills were on repeat prescription and she collected them every week. Surely the doctor should remember how many he dished out. Her mother resented the fact that Thomas lived with Heather. There was a constant conflict between Heather and her mother on what Heather did for everyone else leaving her to struggle. Heather thought her father would have keeled over by now but not, so he was certainly a strong old bugger.

The drugs Thomas took were Tamazapan and Diazepam something called Gabapentin. She thought they were for the treatment of epilepsy there was also something to help him sleep, something for his prostrate, it was all too much. Heather thought her father did not care about his life so maybe she should help him a little.

She experimented with the doses Thomas took. He was supposed to take two of the capsules in the morning with breakfast he often took four then she would add another two to his tea. This didn't make much difference so she added small amounts to his food. She did notice he would then sleep a little longer on a morning and his drinking bouts didn't last as long as he had to come home early from the pub because he was feeling tired. Two weeks later with the extra pills Thomas seemed fine.

Heather got the doctor the following Monday. Thomas hadn't been out of bed for a couple of days he said he felt weak. The doctor asked Thomas about his drinking he of course lied and of course the doctor didn't believe him.

"Thomas this is serious, you can't drink on the medication you take they don't mix" said the Doctor shaking his head at the same time.

"Yes doctor I know but what's there to life, without the sweet taste of whiskey, the doctor and Thomas laughed. It was almost two weeks before Thomas died. He had overdosed on Diazepam and whiskey it had been expected. When the doctor came he spoke to Heather and Jeff "I'm sorry Heather he just wouldn't listen

To me."

"I don't think he would have listened to anyone Doctor he was a man of his own mind." Said Heather sobbing on Jeff's shoulder. Jeff bent towards her and curled his arm around her in an act of affection.

After the funeral Heather decorated the smaller back bedroom in soft greens. She bought new bedding and a bedside lamp it was there that she would often sleep when Jeff's snoring got too much. It was her sanctuary, she had little figures on the window cill and had set her lap top up with a printer and a book case with all her crime favourites, Ian Rankin, Agatha Christie, James Patterson and so many more, Jeff wasn't a reader he was a watcher, a television watcher. The programmes were usually about fishing or reclamation salvage hunters, off Griders in Alaska oh my god.

This little Paradise was where Heather felt alive she read her books and decided that it was possible for someone like her to write. She had tried a few times but then got lost half way through. When you have children and elderly parents to look after you don't have time for anything else and there was her full time job a very important job. One that was supporting them now Jeff had been made redundant.

CHAPTER SEVENTEEN

Heather brought herself back to earth and stared up at her dark haired son Tom he worked for the council in the planning department. He was so handsome; Tom was married to Sarah who had a florist shop on the High street. Sarah was a tall sleek blonde with a wonderful dress sense they had been married about ten years Heather couldn't remember exactly how many but no children. Heather thought it was because she wouldn't want the children putting their dirty paws on their beautiful house. You could tell when they visited as a family when Charlie and Luke appeared Sarah followed them around with a packet of wet wipes. It was true what they say you have a girl all your life you have boy till he finds a wife. How true Tom was the apple of his mother's eye. I want to marry you mummy he used to say then he grew up and loved someone else, forgetting about his mother. The marriage seemed solid enough and the lack of children was never brought up even Jeff didn't make jokes anymore. The party went with a swing.

Jeff got drunk, Iris had three sherries and sang Scarborough Fair. After midnight and champagne the happy throng left to their own homes.

Heather and the team had settled as the threat of redundancy had quietened down. Heather had thought it best to curb her activities for the time being, Maggie's death had been very close to home even more so when Maggie's estate had been settled as Charlie and Luke had been beneficiaries of her will. A trust had been set up for them maturing when they reached 25yrs old. Heather thought that this was only right after the trauma the children had experienced through the actions of their waster of a father.

Heather sat in front of her dressing table her mother's silver mirror and brush set had pride of place she ran her fingers across the silver engraved back of the mirror then slowly turned it around she didn't know what she expected to see. A grey blurred visage no features she blended into the colour of the wallpaper beige her mother would have said beige.

On reaching work she put the kettle on and spooned out coffee into cups ready for staff to arrive. Good mornings went around as each person hung their coats in the staff room.

'Has anyone heard anything from Pam asked Heather staff shook their heads.

'It's not like Pam to miss" said Christine. Heather agreed she rang Pam's home number no answer she looked at records and found Pam's mobile number no answer.

"She will let us know soon I am sure" Heather said and reported the absence to the main office.

The following day there was still no answer from Pam Heather was quite worried it was so unlike her. Pam lived with her partner Natalie in a terraced cottage near the canal. Heather had been there a couple of times to a birthday party and a barbecue. It was only ten minutes away she thought she would go there at lunchtime just to make sure everything was alright.

During the morning Mrs Reed, Pam's mother rang to find out if Pam was at work she had been trying to contact her with no success. Heather told Mrs Reed that she also had been worried about Pam and would go to her house at lunchtime.

Heather walked on the tow path of the canal until she reached the terrace of cottages called Mill Row. The terrace was in fact one house. Pam and Natalie had done a brilliant job of renovating the old terrace into a beautiful home. The couple had been together for five years and had seemed very happy. Heather being old school didn't quite understand the dynamics of a lesbian relationship but it didn't offend her.

It was a lovely sunny day it was good to get out of the Library into the fresh air. She opened the iron gate to the property, it gave a sing song sound as she closed it behind her. The breeze tickled a wind chime, idyllic she thought. Raising the knocker on the door she gave three loud raps. Heather looked at her feet as she waited for the door to open. No answer, she moved towards the tiny mullion windows it seemed very dark inside even though the sun was shining. She noticed a number of blue bottle flies bouncing on the glass panes. Then she saw on the carpet at the side of the sofa a pair of bare legs. Heather knocked on the window "Pam, Pam answer the door "Heather looked up and down the tow path not knowing what to do.

She knew she had to do something so she tried the front door it opened immediately she looked around the lounge everything was neat and pristine she looked at the body on the floor it was Pam she was naked apart from a pair of red silk knickers. Pam's body she was laid in a pool of dark congealed blood. The blood had seeped from the large wound in her neck. Heather was shocked but she was also enthralled. She felt Pam's body it was as cold as ice my god thought Heather who could have done this. She went to the bottom of the stair case.

"Natalie Natalie" she shouted there was no answer, Heather took the handrail and slowly climbed the stairs each step creaked under her feet. As she reached the top of the stairs she quietly called Natalie's name again there was no reply. Shit I don't suppose I should be here she thought but it was too late she was in the heart of a murder scene. The main bedroomed held a beautifully made bed with curtains to match, the bed was topped with satin cushions very tasteful. Heather moved slowly to the en-suite bathroom she found Natalie, who was crumpled in the shower unit. Heather hadn't seen so much blood before. Two large bath towels were in a pile with what looked like a Chinese chopping knife very amateur thought Heather. Yes, Natalie was dead there was a number of large gaping wounds to her body she had struggled that was obvious by the hand marks on the shower wall. Heather felt a little queasy as more flies buzzed around the room. She thought she had better ring the police this was none of her doing and she had to do the right thing.

Using her mobile Heather rang 999 it took almost ten minutes before a police squad car followed by a van and a black car appeared on the scene. Heather stood by the gate as all the people from the vehicles rushed into the cottage after a number of minutes a policeman in uniform came out and stood at the door a woman in a grey trouser suit approached Heather.

"Are you Mrs Foster you found the bodies? Heather acknowledged she was and told the DCI that she was Pam's boss and had been worried about her.

Yes, she had touched the body downstairs to check whether Pam was alive or not. The DCI guided Heather to the black car and sat Heather in the back seat and told her that she should wait there until they could get someone to take her home. Heather asked if she could telephone the council office to let colleagues know she was safe. She was allowed to do this but not to divulge anything that had gone on.

Other vehicles arrived and Heather sat patiently in the back seat of the detectives' car. Well nothing seemed to amaze her, how on earth had she got herself in the middle of this. She was a little worried because no doubt she would have to give her fingerprints to rule her out of this murder. She hoped that she had been very careful from her own activities. Looking back on events she reassured herself that she had planned everything to the minute details, she was a professional. After a couple of hours, the detective came out to the car.

"Sorry to keep you waiting Heather you realise we have a double murder here how are you feeling?" Heather said she would like to return home. DCS Conner said that could be arranged. The detective told Heather that she was stationed at Mapplebeck Police station she gave Heather her card and if she needed she could contact her anytime. It was arranged that one of the uniformed officers took Heather home and a statement would be made the following day. "Is that ok?" She gave Heather a sweet smile.

Jeff shook his head when Heather told him about what had happened, "Bloody hell Heather the police have been to this house more times in the last couple of years than there have been hot dinners." Jeff returned to Discovery Shed and lit a cigarette. Heather had a bath. As she lay in the lovely bubbles she went over the scene in her head. Who would have done such a thing there wasn't anything out of place in the lounge or upstairs so nobody was searching for valuables. It had to be personal, so you had to think friends, family, close acquaintances, this would be unique she could solve a murder instead of murdering someone, yes there are always two sides to a coin.

Heather lit the Gardenia candle at the side of the bath. This was a new feeling she could hear the machinery inside her head chugging away. She could become Miss Marple or Rebus or Scarpetta, she made a list in her head.

Robbery

Sexual motive

Greed

Revenge

Opportunist

Pleasure although she ruled this out as it was so unlikely.

Robbery there was no sign of robbery. Nothing seemed out of place. Pam was very neat and tidy Heather had liked that about her even at the Library, she was constantly putting books away and cataloguing, not like Christine who would never return books to their rightful place. In Heathers mind she walked through the cottage as she had found it. The door wasn't locked so no sign of forced entry. Upstairs nothing was out of place on the dressing table. She could rule out robbery unless it was secret papers or just a single valuable item that the robber knew about. Heather turned the hot tap with her toe and topped the bath up

Sexual motive, Pam was in her knickers which was a little odd as she was downstairs. If there had been anyone at the door surely she would have put on her dressing gown. Maybe when you are liberated and living with another woman you don't need a dressing gown.

Natalie was naked, not a pretty sight with all that blood. Someone didn't like her that was for sure. However, Natalie was still in the shower she hadn't been sexually molested or she couldn't tell if she had been. Someone had crept up on her and savagely stabbed her to death.

It could have been another woman a lesbian threesome gone wrong. No she had to rule sexual motive out maybe put it on the back burner.

Greed, her favourite and favourite among authors worldwide, someone wants something you have, she knew that feeling. Yes, greed was a possibility.

Revenge, Pam and Natalie could have done something to someone and they were angry enough to commit double murder.

Opportunist, a person walking past just happened to see Pam in her knickers opened the front door and killed Pam then Natalie, unlikely.

Heather took another sip of her glass of Chardonnay when she was rudely interrupted by the door handle being rattled.

"What are you doing in there woman?' "You haven't drowned have you? I need to go to the toilet hurry up'

"Jeff you will have to wait I told you I was having a bath."

"Having a bath, you could have swum the English Channel open the door."

Heather reluctantly arose like Venus from the tub and wrapped a fluffy towel around her body and opened the door to the cross legged Jeff.

"About bloody time you need to think about my prostrate' he moaned carrying the Sunday Times Magazine then shutting the door sharply behind him.

After drying herself she put on fresh pyjamas and her dressing gown and laid on her bed. She had a note pad and pen on the bedside table and started to make a list of what she knew about Pam and Natalie.

She had known Pam for almost ten years she was married to Clive then they had a little boy who had tragically died when he was five. Pam and Clive drifted apart as couples often do in such circumstances. Then about five years ago Pam had spoken to Heather in confidence and told her she was seeing a woman, a lesbian. Heather was shocked she had never met a lesbian before and now she had one working with her. When Pam eventually 'came out' to her colleagues she introduced everyone to Natalie a thirty something red head who was very comfortable with her sexuality. They made a good couple bought the old terrace of houses by the canal and over the last few years renovated them to a high standard.

Pam's family had been upset at her new life especially Danny Pam's brother he had been to the library a few times but Heather had also met him at a Christmas party Pam had held at the Terrace. He was drunk and made very rude remarks about Pam and Natalie.

Yes, Danny had to be in the picture he was an oversized spoiled brat. He still lived with his mother in Steeton, a village the other side of Bishop Horton he didn't work, in fact he didn't do anything. Danny claimed that he was a full time carer for his mother but Heather often saw him hanging about The Three Cups or near the market.

CHAPTER EIGHTEEN

What Heather didn't know was that Danny
had killed Pam and Natalie. He had been out on the
Sunday night at The Three Cups and bought some
MKat from Si the local dealer. It was cheap from Si
although you didn't quite know what you were putting
in your body. The substance could have been baking
soda or rat droppings anything but he didn't care he
was sick of living with his mother. He was thirty for
God's sake he hadn't got a thing. A lousy room in a
council house his mother wanting cups of tea
constantly. Go to the shop Danny, fetch this Danny,
get that. His sister was well out of it. Smart arse, she
was mums' favourite sat in that brilliant cottage
surrounded by beautiful things but living with another
woman how bad was that. His mates had mocked him
and made crude remarks. He didn't like it at all. Pam
and Clive were a great couple when they had young
Harry. He was over the moon he had loved that little
boy. He would babysit, take him to football. When
Harry had died no one had asked him how he felt, they
just bothered about Pam. He was crushed and ached

for that little boy. Pam didn't look after him properly he had got meningitis. Pam and Clive had been sent home from the hospital with a couple of pills. They had said he had flu, how could a mother just be turned away why didn't she stand her ground and fight for that poor little boy.

Si had given Danny MKat and some pills that were supposed to be Tramadol with a bit of luck they would make him sleep. He downed the pills with a couple of whiskeys that felt better he had taken £20 from his mother's purse she wouldn't miss it.

"Come back to mine Danny" said Si "I've got a bit of blow and some beers." Danny thought what a good idea. The two stopped at the Chinese take away and bought chow mien and chips then wobbled to Si's room in one of the large houses off Lister Avenue. The place was a hovel a moth eaten cat stretched its matted legs hoping that it would get the scraps of the take away. Si gave Danny a fork from the side of the sink and they ate their supper. This was followed by a bottle of beer and a shot, a shot of what Danny didn't know what, it tasted like puke. Then Si rolled a couple of joints.

"This is good stuff mate it's from Manchester, what do you think?" slurred Si.

"Yeh great" said Danny as his head spun around and the elephants danced with the spiders in the corner of the room.

It must have been about 4.00am when Danny woke blurry eyed he felt sick and was in the waste paper bin at the side of the fireplace. He wiped his mouth then put the kettle on to make a cup of tea. Si was fast asleep in the easy chair. After two cups of tea Danny was feeling a bit better he had to go home his mother would be wondering what on earth had happened to him. Although she knew he often stayed out these days, he didn't really want to go home to that bloody house that smelt of decaying people. Why did he put up with looking after an old lady, no girlfriend, wife or family as such ridiculed by so many in the pub because of his sister, his only mate was Si. He looked at the body laid in the chair opposite. Si's greasy hair hung down his face and there was a loud snoring coming from his whiskered face. There was a bag with two white tablets in. Danny took the tablets and another swig of tea. Fuck me, it was all Pam's fault he had been left with his mother just left. How was he supposed to meet somebody and settle down, the fat lesbian bitch, he ought to make her pay. It shouldn't be him that people ridiculed it should be her and that black bitch she was hooked up with. Danny fastened his belt and put on his jacket. It was light now 6.30am he had decided to sort this out once and for all.

He walked through the market his pace quickening he hadn't noticed the market stall holders getting their stalls ready for market day or people going to work all he had on his mind was his sister. His bitch of a sister how dare she treat him like this. What a mug he had been to stay with his mother so Pam could set up yet another life. He turned onto the canal tow path he could see the terrace there was a light on downstairs and one on in the bedroom upstairs, he walked up to the front door. His heart was beating so fast he thought it was going to explode from his chest. He turned the front door handle it was open, Pam would have let the cat out he stepped inside Pam was in the kitchen she had heard the front door and walked into the lounge, bloody hell thought Danny she only had her knickers on.

"You fucking bitch, I hate you" he shouted, his hand held the knife he had put in his pocket at Si's, he didn't know why he had picked it up but it made him feel safe. "You fucking bitch" he said again.

Pam walked towards him "Danny what's wrong" his eyes burnt into hers what's wrong? She must know what was wrong. He felt the knife for another second then pulled it from his pocket and stuck it into Pam's neck. She gurgled and fell to the floor her eyes were wide open, she looked like a deer in headlights. He left her by the sofa and jumped up the stairs to find Natalie. He could hear water running she was in the shower.

Natalie didn't hear him as she was facing the back of the shower, she turned suddenly as though she felt someone else in the room. She held her arms out as Danny lifted the knife again and again until she crumpled into a heap in the shower tray. The blood swirled around as it went down the plughole. Danny washed his hands and the knife under the spray of the shower his heart was still beating twenty to the dozen, he was a little wet but that would dry in no time he looked about the bedroom. On the bedroom dressing table there were some notes eighty quid, I think that's mine, he said to himself. He stuffed the notes in his pocket and slowly went down the stairs he walked over to Pam's body. He stared at the prostrate body of his beloved sister. She was definitely dead there was now a large pool of dark red blood that had already soaked into the cream carpet.

He heard the cat meowing at the door he looked down at the body again. Pam's mouth was open and there was a little speck of blood on her cheek he moved his gaze from the body to the coffee table nothing to nick there, it was time to go.

He carefully wiped the front door handles and closed the door behind him. He walked up the tow path back through the market and back to Si's house. Si was still fast asleep in the chair he noticed a big pile of dirty washing in a basket in the kitchen. He took his tee shirt off that had specks of blood on the front of it and picked a black tee shirt from the basket. He wasn't sure if it was clean or dirty. It did smell but he put it on, then his jacket over the top. Danny made another cup of tea and watched breakfast television until Si woke about 10.00am "Morning mate do you want a cuppa?' Si grunted and nodded his head "you're awake early."

"I've just woken that stuff last night was mean, what was in it?"

"Good stuff mate good stuff' they both laughed.

"I need to go home; it's been a good session we will have to do it again soon" joked Danny

"Sure thing mate sure thing" nodded Si lighting up a cigarette, "you don't want another drag?"

"Well why not it would be a shame not too" Danny took his jacket off and rolled a joint the two men drew long and hard, nice. Danny was surprised Si hadn't noticed that he was wearing his tee shirt thank goodness. Danny stayed at the house until lunch time then said he would have to go home to sort his mother out.

When Danny got home his mother had managed to get out of bed herself and was downstairs sat in front of the television eating a toasted crumpet and drinking a mug of tea.

"Where have you been Danny I have been shouting you for the last two hours its bloody mean leaving me like that" she moaned. It was amazing wasn't it she had managed. Danny looked at the frail old woman sitting in the chair.

"Stop lecturing me I have had enough; I can never do anything right".

He fell to his knees before his mother and sobbed.

"Danny what's wrong, it's alright I managed it was hard but I managed what's wrong?"

Danny had his head in his mother's lap and cried for Pam and Natalie and for himself.

"I'm going to ring Pam she needs to come over" his mother said

"No you don't have to do that I'm alright I stopped at Si's last night I had too much to drink I'm tired" he sniffed and wiped his nose on his sleeve.

"Make yourself a cup of tea and go to bed for a few hours and we will have some fish and chips for tea." She stroked his head.

He smiled fish and chips a reward for murdering his sister.

Danny went to bed with his Star Wars mug of steaming tea. His mother reached for the phone at her side she rang Pam's number the phone rang out; she would be working but Natalie should have been there. She thought she would ring later after five. She opened her phone book maybe just try her mobile, she pressed the numbers carefully why were they so long. No answer the voice on the other end asked her to leave a message.

"Hello Pam it's your mum I need to speak to you about Danny get back to me as soon as possible, love you" she hated answer phones but she was sure she had done it right. She heard Danny getting into bed, what had happened, something was wrong.

Danny pulled the covers over his head how could he get out of this it wouldn't be long before someone found the bodies. It was Pam's fault she had asked for this.

Two days had passed and Danny's mother had not heard from Pam. Danny wouldn't go to the house she wasn't sure what to do. Looking through her phone book there was the number for the Bishop Horton Library. Mrs Reed rang the number.

"Bishop Horton Library how can I help you"

"Hello my name is Mrs Reed can I speak to Heather Fosters please?"

"Yes of course just one moment please" there was a silence then Heather answered the phone.

"Hello Mrs Reed I am so pleased you have rung I was getting worried about Pam"

Mrs Reeds voice sounded so frail.

"Oh no I thought you may have known what has happened to her it's so unlike her she hasn't rung or called in I am so worried.

"I agree Mrs Reed, look I will pop down to the cottage at lunchtime there could be a very simple answer, I will get her to ring as soon as possible"

"Thank you Mrs Foster I am so grateful" Mrs Reed had a dreadful feeling.

CHAPTER NINETEEN

The police knocked on Danny Reeds door his mother shouted Danny from the lounge.

"Danny door" Danny was washing cups in the sink he dried his hands as the person at the door rapped again.

"Danny" his mother shouted again.

"I am going I'm going" Danny's worst nightmare was stood on the step in front of him. A policeman in uniform and two women who showed their warrant cards DC Shaw and DSI Phillips

"Hello Mr Reed may we come in please we need to speak to you and your mother" the three moved forward and Danny indicated the door they should take.

"Mum it's the police, they want to speak to us" Mrs Reed put her hand to her heart.

"Oh no, I knew there was something wrong. Its Pam isn't it she's had an accident. Oh Danny, Danny what's happened what's happened" her eyes questioned each person in the room.

"There is no other way to say this Mrs Reed your daughter and her partner have been found at their cottage dead, we believe in suspicious circumstances.

"Oh no" uttered Danny and put his head in his hands

"No No "cried Mrs Reed "Not Pam"

Danny put his arms around his mother

"Shh Shh mum" Danny comforted her.

The detectives asked questions, when they had last seen Pam or Natalie and when did they last have any contact with the couple. They asked about the relationship they had with both of the deceased. Mother and son said that they loved Pam and Natalie. Danny explained that he had stayed at his friends Tuesday and Wednesday nights although he had been home in between to check on his mother. His mother gave him a sideward glance. She didn't contradict Danny but started to sob loudly.

DC Shaw suggested that the family doctor be called and maybe the neighbour could come around to sit with her while Danny went with them to the mortuary where he could identify the bodies. Danny said that he couldn't do it but the detectives insisted that it was something necessary. Danny's heart was beating fast he could feel the eyes of the detectives burn into his body as they watched his every movement. He thought he had murderer written across his forehead.

The dark haired one didn't speak it was the blonde haired one that seemed in charge she was like a terrier one question after another. Danny stuck to his story of being at Si's admitting he had taken drugs and was drunk. DC Shaw recognised the signs of abuse and wondered if she was looking at the person who had killed the two women.

Danny was ushered into the mortuary he didn't know if he would be able to stand this. His head was spinning at the thought of seeing his dead sister. The curtain was drawn back and he saw the two gurneys with the bodies of Pam and Natalie. The sheets were pulled up to their chins. He didn't see his dirty deed. They looked asleep not dead they could have jumped up and shouted surprise, he made a jerking motion as though frightened out of his skin. He crumpled onto the floor crying the officer at his side helped him up.

"I'll take you home Danny we can talk later. Come on you need to look after your mother she needs you now "DC Shaw put her arm around him and led him to the door. He was dropped at home a liaison officer stayed with him and his mother for a while before leaving the sad household.

CHAPTER TWENTY

When officers returned to the police station they created a theatre of events with a time line on a large white board.

Rachel said, "Danny looks a possible suspect. Drug fuelled attack what do you think?"

Abby looked at the notes before her, "He looks like a mummy's boy to me, not much of a carer leaving his mother alone at night."

"Yet mum was able to get out of bed and sort herself out all by herself, not that disabled".

Both women went into the boss's office, Chief Inspector Baron nodded to his two detectives

"Well Sherlock and Watson whose done it?"

"Early doors yet boss but the brothers story is a bit weak there doesn't seem to be anyone else in the picture.

"Well get him in and put the pressure on let's wrap it up quick Bishop Horton is too nice a place for murder."

The doctor had been to the house and Mrs Reed was in bed under sedation. The neighbour who had been sitting with her went home. After the police liaison officer left for the evening Danny held his head in his hands. What had he done his bloody sister was still causing him grief. He needed something he felt so bad he had to find Si and get some gear. He listened at the foot of the stairs he could hear the low snoring of his mother deep in sleep. Slowly he opened the door expecting a policeman to be stood on the doorstep but there was no one there. The government cuts had reached Bishop Horton as in the rest of the country. The door gave a quiet click, he was free. He walked down passed the market place and on to The Three Cups he occasionally looked behind him just in case the police had been watching him all the time and were following him.

As he entered the bar he saw Si and Alan sat in the corner.

"God Danny didn't think you would be here tonight, fucking hell that is awful about Pam and Nat who could have done something like that?" asked Si.

"I had to get out Si there are so many weirdos about these days it could have been anyone"

Si nodded in agreement.

"It wasn't bloody me" said Alan finishing off a pint of Guinness, Danny gave him a look of disgust.

"What do you want mate? I'm buying "Alan gathered the two glasses and waited for Danny's order. As Alan stood at the bar Danny turned towards Si.

"Si I need something I feel crap have you got anything?" He looked like frightened rabbit.

"I've got some good stuff, near pure but it's a little more expensive I would like to give you it cheap but I have to buy it too." Si was all heart.

"Corse I have money" Danny pulled two twenty notes out of his back pocket.

"Fucking hell Danny you're flush "said Si.

"Yeh me mum felt sorry for me" Danny exchanged the forty pounds for two small bags of cocaine and baking soda.

"Stop for a drink Danny" said Alan he had brought three large whiskies to the table.

"Cheers" said Danny and threw the burning liquid to the back of his throat. He said his goodbyes and took his self-home.

Danny stopped in the market place and found a barren stall away from the road to lay two lines of the white powder he couldn't wait until he got home he needed it now. The snowy white dust was gone in a breath. He immediately felt better fresh clear headed things seemed more in prospective, he needed a plan.

When he got home his mother was still sound asleep he tiptoed into his bedroom giggling he switched his Xbox on and played his favourite game of soldiers on a killing spree.

The following morning his mother was very quiet bursting into tears occasionally. Bloody hell how long was this going to go on for. He made constant cups of tea for her and neighbours who thought it would be ok to call in. He was bloody sick of it.

"Well at least you have your Danny looking after you" said Mrs Robbins from across the road, Danny thought she was being sarcastic.

"Yes I suppose but a son isn't like a daughter is it. Pam was so good to me I don't know what I am going to do without her." His mother started to cry again.

"Mrs Robbins I think my mum needs a rest", he said and opened the lounge door, Mrs Robbins sniffed, and left as she opened the front door the blonde detective stood on the step she smiled at the neighbour as she passed her.

Danny's heart hit the floor of his stomach he was going to be sick they had come for him.

"What's wrong "he stuttered

"Nothing Mr Reed are you ok?. asked DC Shaw "I have just come to see if you and your mother are alright, we have made an appointment down at the station for you tomorrow if that's alright with you. We do need to ask you a few more questions so we can piece things together say three o'clock?" she was so bright why was she so bright.

"I suppose so" his mind twisting and turning they must know they must.

"We are doing our best to find whoever did this dreadful thing Mr Reed I promise you "DC Shaw looked into his eyes.

"I am sure you are" agreed Danny. The detective had a few words with his mother and left asking him to ring if he needed anything.

He watched the detective return to her car from behind the curtain in the lounge.

"What are you doing with those curtains you're like a peeping tom put them down" yelled his mother.

"I need to go out and do a bit of shopping" said Danny

"Oh yes leave me all by myself you don't care about me. Having my life turned upside down, I might as well be dead for all you care, I would be with Pam then. I haven't got anything to live for" she raised her arms in the air then clutched at her ample bosom I don't suppose I have long anyways with all this stress."

Danny didn't answer her he just slammed the door after himself.

He walked to The Three Cups and sat on the benches outside he looked around there wasn't anyone about. He folded a business card he had in his pocket it was advertising the local taxi cab Fast Carz 668866 he giggled a little as he pushed the other packet of white powder in the crevice then sniffed loudly drawing the mixture into his already buzzing nasal capacity.

Wow he was here, alive at last, he was the man he hadn't felt this good for so long, he couldn't be locked up for life it was bad enough with his mother. He was like a caged animal. He wondered if the police knew it was him he had spent a few hours of questioning had he given anything away. The blood in the shower running down the plughole just like in Physco. He held the picture in his head. He didn't have to kill Natalie it would have been better not to have. She would have discovered Pam's body then she may have been charged with the murder. That was a missed opportunity.

He went into the pub there were a few acquaintances at the bar he nodded and looked in the corner of the room where Si sat alongside a girl with straggly hair.

"Thanks Si" she giggled and tucked the small plastic bag into her anorak pocket. She squeezed past Danny.

"Sorry about your sister Danny "she bowed her head feeling embarrassment.

"Yeah thanks" said Danny feeling the same embarrassment.

"My man Danny boy ,you looked stoked"

"Yeah some of your prime but I need some more. He reached into his pocket and drew out another forty pounds.

"You are flushed these days" Si stuck the notes in the top pocket of his shirt.

"Here you are mate best customer of the day and here a couple of tabs on the house so to speak"

"Thanks Si I just need to get this shit out of my head."

"Here, have a good night doctor Si's orders" he handed him another couple of tablets.

Danny took them not even asking what they were. He put them with the rest of his stash.

"Are you going to have a beer Dan?"

"No thanks I need to go home to make sure me mums ok she's in a bit of a state.

"Yeh course see you later" Si went to the bar and Danny left by the back door.

Everything was clear now he had to leave Bishop Horton he had to leave his mother's house he had to make it on his own in the world he was thirty for God's sake he would go to Manchester or London he could get a job there easy on the black. Disappear into the universe no one to bother him. No running errands for his mother. He needed money though, where was he going to get that.

He opened the front door trying to be as quiet as possible, the hallway clock chimed loudly.

"Is that you Danny" his mother called from her armchair.

"Yes, it is" he walked into the lounge the gas fire was on full blast.

"It's like an oven in here mum" said Danny turning the gas fire down.

"I feel the cold you will too when you get to my age "she pulled her cardigan closer to her body.

"Just make me a cup of tea and take it up for me I'm going back to bed with one of those pills the doctor gave me" she shuffled to the edge of the chair.

Danny made the tea and placed it on the bedside table. He slipped his hand under the mattress and pulled out a handful of notes, his luck was in, three hundred quid. He stuffed the money into his back pocket making sure the bed covers were back nice and neat.

"Are you ready mum?" he shouted down the stairs.

"Yes give me a hand then" Danny helped his mother up the stairs and onto her bed. He unfastened her bra, Mrs Reed had no thoughts about revealing her wrinkled body.

"Oh it's so good to get that off "she scratched her round belly and held her arms up as Danny opened her nightdress dropping it down over her body, there was a faint smell of urine and old body odour.

"We need to get you into the shower tomorrow mum with some of that nice coconut gel."

"Yes but I'm not washing me hair the curls are still springy" she bounced the grey curls on her head.

His mother laid in her bed she had a sip of the tea at her side.

"Lovely, but Pam could make the best cup of tea, who do you think could have done it Danny who could have hurt Pam and Natalie" she sobbed and took another sip of tea.

"I miss her so much she was the best daughter anyone could ask for. She did everything for me if it hadn't been for her I don't know what I would have done."

Danny's jaw dropped, "What about me mum?"

"What about you, you are a waste of space Danny, you are never here when I need you. Always down at that bloody pub. Stealing out of my purse any opportunity, I don't know why I ever had you."

Danny stood above his mother and put his hands around her neck. He snorted with anger as the heat flowed down his arms to his fingertips squeezing as hard as he could.

"You bitch" he said through clenched teeth.

Mrs Reeds eyes bulged out of her head.

No Danny, she couldn't speak but she saw the anger and the hatred in her son's eyes.

CHAPTER
TWENTY ONE

It took Danny a few minutes before he could leave hold of his mother's neck. Her body thudded into the pillow, the cup and saucer fell to the floor. He sat on the bed shaking then sobbed as he realised what he had done. After all he had done he was still only second best. He lifted the mattress there was more money. Twenty and ten pound notes and with one swift motion gathered what he thought was his rightful property. He had to go as quick as possible. Where was he going was anybody's guess. The police would be back tomorrow when he didn't turn up to the station they would then add two and two together and bingo.

He counted the money out on the kitchen table two thousand six hundred pounds. He had struggled on benefits for so long and his mother had been sat on all this money. He went to his mother's black mock crocodile handbag and found another forty pounds. He left the hallway light on so not to arouse suspicion, took his best jacket and headed in the direction of The Three Cups.

He bought himself a large whiskey at the bar then sat in the corner where Si was nursing a pint of beer.

"Bloody hell your poked" said Si looking at the large whiskey Danny was nursing.

"It's for medicinal purposes only, I feel crap" Danny slugged the whiskey down.

"What you need is a taste of special mate."

"I reckon I do" Danny peeled a couple of twenty pound notes from the wad in his pocket. He was clever enough not to pull out all his cash out in front of Si not that he didn't trust him.....but he didn't.

"I might be going to London to work" blurted out Danny.

Si looked at him out of the corner of his eye.

"What about your old mum Danny?"

"She has to go into a home with all this shit it's just tipped her over the edge" Danny stared at the floor

"Have they got any idea whose done it "questioned Si.

"No, no idea, not that I care about the pair of lezzie bitches."

"Yeh know what you mean that was a surprise to everyone about your Pam, even fancied her myself you know older woman and all that."

"You didn't do it did you Danny?" straight out of the blue Si confronted him.

"What kill my own sister what are you on?"

Si saw the look Danny gave him.

"You bloody well did didn't you, bloody hell Danny" Si bent forward Danny closed into the middle of the table.

"I had to do it Si, she was mocking me. What was I supposed to do. She said she was going to tell mum about the drugs and where I got them from. Danny wanted to let Si know he was involved and that he would be willing to help him even if was to save his own skin.

"Calm down mate I can help you get away for a price of course everything costs as well you know."

Danny held his head in his hands.

Si took the glasses "I'll get us a couple of drinks and speak to a mate of mine."

"Don't go telling anyone else I'm in enough shit as it is"

"Trust me mate" Si said as he went to the bar.

Was he really his mate Danny thought. What the fuck had he got himself into. Si returned to the table he had rung the mate and they would meet the following day.

"You can come to mine tonight we can have a good smoke make you feel better. What about your old mum she won't ring the police worried about you will she?"

"No Mrs Robbins is with her tonight she will make sure she's in bed and locked up" Danny looked at the floor not to give away his other secret.

Danny and Si staggered to Si's hovel with a curry and chapattis. They ate their supper. The scraggy cat licking the lid that had been thrown on the floor. Si had created a new bong out of a plastic cola bottle and they both took turns in inhaling. It wasn't long before Si collapsed in front of the television set. Danny watched as Si's body collapsed like a pack of cards. He threw the bong down he couldn't do anymore. He was so tired, he lay down in the armchair and let sleep engulfed his body. The cat ate the remaining curry from the container.

Next morning Danny got up and swilled his face in the dirty sink he wasn't sure whether to wipe his face on the dirty yellow towel or just use his tee shirt he opted for the tee-shirt. Gawd Si was the biggest drug dealer in the county yet he lived like a pig where did all the money go. Si wouldn't wake up for hours. Danny combed his hair and decided to go for a paper and some cigarettes. He walked through the market and onto the High Street he felt like shit.

"Danny Danny" he heard the voice behind him he looked back but didn't recognise anyone. Then a hand touched his shoulder.

"It's Heather, I was Pam's boss we have met a couple of times over the years" her hand was still on his shoulder.

The older woman smiled at him, a kind motherly smile.

"Oh yes I am sorry I'm not really with it" he mumbled Heather had to agree with him there. He smelt of whisky and curry and most of that was on his tee shirt, chicken tikka by the looks of it.

"We are all devastated at the library, Pam was such a wonderful person and a great member of staff. "How are you bearing up. Caring for your mother can't be easy, I know how difficult it can be. My mother in law lives with us she had a stroke so is now bedridden."

It was the first time anyone had asked him he stared at Heather as though in a daze then started to cry.

"OH look Danny, Christine is opening up this morning I will give her a quick ring to say I have been held up and we can go on to the Bluebird for a nice coffee."

Heather used her mobile, Christine was intrigued but took the role of under manager seriously however the whole of the council would know in half an hour that Heather would be in later that morning. Heather didn't care this poor lad needed her.

They sat in the corner of the cafe with two cups of cappuccino and two toasted teacakes.

"How's your mum doing Danny?" asked Heather.

"She's not doing too well, all this has tipped her over the edge she might have to go into a home." Danny stared at the floor

"It must be tough on you too. Its hard work being a carer you never get any thanks do you?"

Danny lifted his head to this grey woman, "Your right nobody thinks about what you want."

No one ever thinks about you this woman knew. Danny started to sob into the paper napkin from his plate.

"Come on Danny things will get better" Heather tapped his arm.

"Nothing is going to get better" he looked again at the grey woman before him.

"The police will help you I am sure they have liaison officers don't they to assist you with all the formalities."

"Nobody has been near, they came to do a couple of statements then nothing I am supposed to go there this afternoon" Heather looked into the face of a young man who was clearly on some sort of drug he could barely join in the conversation just stirring his spoon around and around in his cup.

"Danny are you alright?" Heather asked again.

"Heather I have done something wrong" Danny whispered.

Heather whispered back, "What have you done" but she knew what he had done he didn't have to say anything else.

"Something very wrong"

"You can tell me Danny" Heather spoke in a low voice.

"I have killed three people" his voice was so quiet that Heather had to strain her ears.

"Three people Danny who" Heather was surprised at three.

Danny didn't answer he stared into his coffee cup. Heather was impress three people she only knew of the two.

"Pam and Natalie but who else?" Danny raised his eyes they met Heathers he smiled at her,

"You have really shiny eyes my old mum had shiny eyes" he stirred the empty cup again. Bloody hell his mother, sister, and partner.

Heather had stopped being impressed. Danny was on some sort of drug he had killed a very good person. Pam was competent how could he kill her. She could understand the mother being a carer was so hard and his mother did have a bit of a whiny voice.

"You need to go to the police you need to tell them what you have done."

"They can't lock me up Heather I'll go mad. He felt into his pocket and pulled out a number of small plastic bags Heather recognized the bags from the market stall.

"What are they for Danny" she whispered

"I can't go to the police they won't understand me Heather they won't understand why I did it."

"Why did you Danny" Heather was interested

"Cos she had it all and I had nothing she had two goes two bites of the cherry, she killed my nephew they didn't look after him properly."

"That's not true Danny he had meningitis."

"No they left the hospital they should have stayed they should have demanded" he banged the table and a couple who were sat by the window looked over Heather smiled at them.

Heather had to do something but what, she could ring the police then what would they do. They

142

would put him in Broadmoor or some other mental hospital he would then serve a couple of years and be a drain on society nothing for murdering his family.

"You need to give yourself up Danny" she whispered again

"No No I can't."

Heather felt a little sorry for him but that soon passed. He was a drug addict who just took from everyone and never gave anything back. All the hard earned money she had put into the system to fund his habit. She had to think quickly there was work to go to and last thing she wanted was to be involved with a triple murder. The police must be watching him she had guessed who had done Pam's murder immediately surely they must be a step behind her.

Danny was self-absorbed Heather finished her coffee then bent down and opened her handbag she felt for the pill bottle that contained the heart pills from her mother. It was lucky she always carried them with her, she didn't want Jeff to come across them and wonder why she hadn't taken them to the chemist.

"Danny you could take a couple of these they used to be my mother's they will help you relax they are not very strong if you need to sleep. I know how important that is nobody knows. You will probably be able to think straight, then if you want me to go with you to the police station I will." Heather had removed the top from the bottle.

Danny stared at Heather then held one hand out, Heather tipped a dozen of the tiny blue pills into his hand.

"You can take up to three of these at a time my mum did" she screwed the top back on the bottle and returned it to her handbag. She glanced around the cafe no one was paying any attention to them. Danny put the pills into his pocket. That's right a good night's sleep it's what he needed he just wanted to pull the covers over his head and forget about everything.

"Thanks Heather" he scrapped his chair back. The noise was like chalk on a blackboard.

"I'm going to my mate's house are you going to the police?" his eyes searched Heathers.

"No Danny I will let you come to that decision it would be better for you to hand yourself in."

Danny put his arms around Heather she stood back and stiffly patted his back.

On the High Street they waved goodbye to each other. Heather went to the library and explained to Christine that she had met Danny and what a terrible state he was in and why she had taken him for a coffee. She didn't mention the confession but thought it was prudent to let her know she had seen him.

"Heather you are so kind only you would do that for a druggie" Heather gave her a knowing smile and went about her business.

Danny could feel the pills in his pocket God knows what they were, some sort of sleeping pill he supposed at least he didn't have to pay for them. What did worry him was that he had confessed to Heather. Heather hadn't batted an eyelid; she was a really nice old woman. He did need to sleep he couldn't get the face of his mother out of his mind.

Oh my God his own mother. He got to Si's house and walked straight inside.

"Hi mate you're up early" the scruffy Si said.

"Hi just went for a walk can I have a kip for a bit?"

"Sure you can, do you need anything I have got some premium if you need a buzz?"

"I don't know about a buzz but I need something" Si passed him the pipe he had lit and Danny smoked the crack in it. He then downed the dozen pills Heather had given him with a couple of swigs from the bottle of bourbon.

Danny fell face first into the sofa Si laughed.

"Get up ya beast give us a taste" Si took the bottle from Danny and poured the liquid down his throat it burnt but tasted good.

Danny started to cough he felt a warm tingling feeling in his hands then his arms he had a flash of his mother's face she was bending down and picking him up when he had fallen off the swings in Horton Park.

"Where's my bonny lad" she said "come on sweetheart" she wrapped her bony arms around him. He could smell the faint aroma of lily of the valley she smiled into his eyes and he smiled back.

"Mum I love you" he said. His mother's face changed from the smiling visage to two dark fiery eyes her cheeks shot flames outward and there was a roaring in his ears as he tried to coordinate his arms and legs, he had to get up. Inside his body his heart had grown larger he could feel it trying to burst from his chest, his ears popped as the pain wrecked his drugged torso.

Danny managed to clutch his chest the last movement he would ever make.

Si finished the bottle of bourbon and collapsed in the chair unaware his mate was dead at the side of him.

CHAPTER
TWENTY TWO

Heather was a little worried, what if someone had seen her with Danny. The police would take no time at all to find out about his mother's death or that he had killed his sister and partner. Heather would have to make a decision, she knew Danny wasn't going to last long with the way he was abusing his body, young people these days.

The following morning was Heathers morning off she told Jeff she was going to see the police and let them know she had met Danny. Jeff told her she was stupid the lad had been high on drugs. Things were best left alone didn't she think it was better to forget it, they had been involved so many times with the police over the last few years. But Heather knew she had to cover her own back.

She walked into Bishop Horton main police station. The desk officer asked her what her she wanted then he asked her to take a seat. He held the card Heather had given him with Detective Shaw's name and contact number on. Rachel Shaw opened the interview room door and asked Heather to come in and sit down. Another adjoining door opened and Abby Phillips entered carrying a file under her arm.

"Hello Mrs Foster how can we help you? Have you remembered something? The desk officer says you are worried." Heather composed herself.

"Well its Danny, Danny Reed I met him yesterday on the High Street. He was so upset he looked a bit drunk. I suppose he could have been if your sister had just being murdered" Heather took a deep breath.

"Well he said he had killed three people" Heather sat back in her chair.

"Three people?" the detectives looked at each other.

"Yes three he said, he had killed Pam, Natalie and his mother"

"Why didn't you come yesterday Mrs Foster" asked one of the surprised detectives.

"Well I thought he was drunk, then after work when I got home I told my husband, he said I was being stupid and the lad was out of his head on drugs, he is well known for it."

Both detectives looked at her incredulous, "so why have you come Mrs Foster" said Abby.

"I couldn't sleep last night it was praying on my mind what if he had been telling the truth. So I came here as soon as I could" Heather felt satisfied with her story. "I know Danny he couldn't do such a thing but then again we don't really know a person do we?"

"No" they both echoed

"We will ask you to return home Mrs Foster we need to find Danny I suppose you don't know where he is?"

"At home I expect although he hangs about the Three Cups the public house near the market. Heather picked up her handbag from the floor and followed Rachel and Abby to the foyer.

"We will be in touch with you Mrs Foster thank you for coming you did the right thing. The two detectives collected their car keys and with a uniformed officer went to Danny Reed's home. There was no answer to the loud knocking that the uniformed officer made. The light was on in the hallway but there was no sign of life. The next door neighbour Glenda Smith poked her head out to see what all the noise was about.

"Danny's not in I saw him go out yesterday he hasn't come back" she folded her arms in front of her.

"I think it's disgraceful leaving his poor mother all night by herself, it's a good job she isn't totally disabled, he gets carers allowance for her as well, disgraceful."

"Thank you madam" said Rachel

"There's a key under the plant pot if you need to get in its there just in case."

In case of what thought Abby. Rachel picked up the flower pot and there resting in the dark earth was a key on a Star Wars key ring. Rachel opened the front door.

"Mrs Reed Mrs Reed" Abby opened the lounge door no one. The kitchen was empty there was a solitary spoon and dried up tea bag on the draining board.

"Mrs Reed" Abby called again. The three police officers climbed the stairs slowly this wasn't looking good the first bedroom door was open and there was a smell of sweaty socks and mould. They all crept across the landing

"Mrs Reed" Rachel called again. She opened the bedroom door Mrs Reeds body was laid in the bed the duvet was pulled up to her chin. She was dead Rachel was certain, Abby with one finger pulled the duvet down just enough to see the red and blue marks on her neck, Mrs Reeds tongue was slightly out as though mocking the officers.

"Oh God" said "Rachel we need forensics here asap and we need to find Danny Reed."

"Do you think he did his sister and partner as well?" asked Abby

"Looks like it"

The uniformed officer radioed for crime scene officers while Rachel and Abby looked around the house for clues as to where Danny could be

"I'll go next door and find out if Mrs Nosey neighbour knows his mates" said Rachel

Mrs Smith didn't know Danny's mates but she did know he frequented the Three Cups in town.

"He is always there with his druggie friends disgraceful."

Other officers had arrived at the house, photographs and forensics were in place as Rachel and Abby sped off to the Three Cups. They arrived with a few drinkers hung about the bar. Abby spoke to the barman while Rachel spoke to some of the customers. One young woman swung her ponytail.

"Yeh I know Danny he's always in here he has loads of mates but he usually sits with Si, yes Si Pinter he lives on Wellington Avenue near the football pitch. I don't know what number it is but it's got a bloody awful yellow door." Both Rachel and Abby thought the young girl was more than likely to be a customer of Sis.

Both officers got into the car and headed for Wellington Avenue. The avenue consisted of large Victorian houses most had been converted into bedsits or flats what once had been very beautiful architectural designed homes with pretty front gardens they were now run down properties with overgrown gardens or yards, dustbins spilled their contents out on to pathways. They didn't have to look for long the khaki yellow door was third after the football pitch there was a large number forty-five painted in red on the letter box.

"Let's hope he is here" said Rachel she knocked on the door as they both stood in anticipation on what was on the other side.

The door opened slowly they held their ID cards up.

"I didn't do anything, how did you know, I didn't do it" Si sounded frightened he was dressed in a pair of shorts with no shirt. He opened the door wider and allowed the officers to enter.

"He was like that this morning I couldn't wake him; I was going to ring you."

"Well you didn't have to, we are here."

They looked down at the body of Danny Reed he was laid on his back there was a stain of vomit on his tee-shirt, in death he looked frightened and forgotten just the way he had led his life.

Rachel felt Danny's neck he was cold. Reading Si his rights he was then taken to the police station protesting his innocence all the way.

CHAPTER
TWENTY THREE

All in all Heather was pleased with the outcome. The main drug dealer in Bishop Horton had been locked up now that was true justice. A murderer had been despatched no costly imprisonment it had saved the judiciary millions as they no longer had to pay trial fees. Yes things had gone well. She put down the newspaper, reading the updates on Simon Pinter drug Baron. He had been charged with the ma with a cigarette he took turns in slurping his tea and puffing on his roll up.

Iris was sat up in bed switching channels with the remote. She asked Heather for a biscuit.

"Have we got any chocolate ones?"

"Sorry mum Jeff has had the last one"

Iris tutted and dipped the plain digestive into her tea with her good hand.

"Fish for tea" chirped Heather trying to make a bad situation better.

"Nice"

Things were sorted. Heather left her watching Countdown. After the fish supper things were washed and put away the doorbell rang. It was the care team who had come to give Iris her bath before bed. Heather was so pleased she didn't have to do this, she had done it for her own mother but didn't think it was right to do it for her mother in law there was enough fetching and carrying to do.

She thought about her own mother in the tiny bungalow surrounded by junk. She would have to squeeze past piles of books and boxes of knitting wools all ready for the next project. Heathers mother was very demanding, why is it that as people got older they insisted it was done their way and when they wanted it. She supposed it was right although here she was almost sixty and still not in charge of her own life.

There were some fond memories of her mother all those knitted jumpers even the knitted swimsuit that when wet doubled in size causing many embarrassing moments. As Heather laughed inside at the spectacle. A dark mist then filled her mind of the last few days of her mother's life. Her mother had Angina and other ailments too many to remember. Her mother had suffered an attack of her angina and Heather found her on the floor in the kitchen. Mum had a mobile phone with just Heathers number in it. She had rung Heather at work saying she didn't feel well then Heather had rung an ambulance to meet her at the bungalow. She was taken to the hospital with Heather following in a taxi. Mrs Blair refused to stay in hospital or go to Heathers she wanted to go home. If she was going to die she wanted to be surrounded by her own things not in Heathers surgically clean house.

"Who is going to look after you mum?" asked Heather.

"You are aren't you "her mother barked. "You managed to look after your father."

"I have to go to work mum it's a very important part of the year for us." Said Heather feeling the guilt.

"You work in the library Heather not the United Nations."

"I might be able to get a few days off but I still say you should be in hospital"

"Oh shut up if you can't be here I'll manage thousands do, I only thought as your mother you would care a bit about me "then ended with "In my last days."

Heather stared at her, creaking gate more like.

Heather took leave from work and spent the next few days ferrying back and forth to her mother's home. The doctor had called and given Heather a prescription for a morphine based medicine alongside her usual drugs.

"It will make her a bit sleepy but she needs a rest."

"She thinks she is going to die doctor" said Heather showing concern.

"Oh we are all going to die Heather, what's the saying, 'Like a thief in the night' we never know when our times up, she is very ill though and how old is she?"

"Eighty-six."

"Well there you go she's had a good innings." The doctor packed his bag.

Heather was surprised of how flippant he was but she didn't know what was going to happen. How long would she be off work they needed her, why was everything always left for her to sort out. Women never had time to themselves unless they were eighty-six of course.

She gave her mother the medicine and gazed upon the face that had lived almost a century. She thought her mother had been very beautiful when she was a young woman. There were photographs of her when she was a land girl sat upon a tractor. There was a wedding photo taken at St Stephens Church in West Bowling two young people staring into the camera a whole life before them. Heather looked from the wedding photograph in the silver frame to the wizened body laid in the bed. There had been a lot of life in between.

Muriel Blair was tired very tired. The doctors medicine had worked she felt at ease. Heather didn't understand you couldn't do all the things you wanted to when you are old and decrepit. Most daughters moved their elderly parents in with them things had changed from her day. Heather had her mother in law living in one bedroom why couldn't she have the other. Her daughter stood above the bed watching her.

"Heather why are you looking at me like that stop staring?"

Heather smiled, "It's alright mum I'm here, it's alright."

"I know you are bloody there, I'm not blind you are so stupid sometimes. Put another cover over me I'm cold."

Heather remembered as she pulled the cover up over the frail body her mother's eyes closed she raised her hand. Heather put her hand over it they were the same shape. Her own nails painted a pale pink they had not always been like that. As a child she had bitten them to the quick, her mother painting bitter aloes upon them so she would not chew them. It was part of being a woman beautiful nails. She dropped her mother's hand to the bed and stood.

The doctor arrived later that day and signed the death certificate.

"Well Heather they say that you know when you are going and she was right wasn't she, are you alright?"

Heather sniffed she thanked the doctor and saw him out allowing the funeral directors to come in and remove the body.

CHAPTER
TWENTY FOUR

Iris wanted to go to Claire and Mikes wedding and she wanted a new outfit, Jeff said he couldn't take her it was something a woman had to do. Claire was too busy to help out so Heather had to take Iris on Saturday afternoon after work. Iris was donned out in a pale blue skirt and jacket with beige shoes and handbag it wasn't going to be a church do so there was no need for a hat.

Heather had bought a very nice navy blue suit with a white blouse she didn't really want to splash out but it was an occasion and there wasn't many of those these days.

She sat in the garden that evening it was warm for September and she had poured herself a large gin and tonic, ice and lemon, luxury but she deserved it. She could hear Jeff talking with his mother the bedroom window was open.

"Are you sure you want to go to this wedding mum, it's going to be a long day for you?"

Heather could imagine Iris trying to communicate as best she could with Jeff and him ignoring and signs she gave.

Heather knew he didn't want her to go it would mean that he would have to be responsible for her at some time.

Heather wondered if Jeff would look after her if she was ill. Over the years if she had a cold or once when she had flu she was left in bed for days without Jeff even trying to make a meal or looking after her at all. When did it all change she reflected on the passing years when she was Hev. Even Jeff called her Hev in their early years when had it changed to Heather probably when she had become invisible.

However, being invisible had its rewards as she remembered the body of Sam and the blood on the carpet.

Jeff joined her in the garden.

"Mums not sure if she will be able to go to the wedding having a bit of trouble with her leg"

"She has a wheelchair Jeff"

"I know that but we don't really want to be pushing it about all day" Jeff went inside to take his position in front of the television.

Heather had no words for him she sipped her gin and thought why had she been with Jeff for so long, he didn't care about her he didn't even care about his own mother. As the sun set in the garden there was a shout from inside

"Are we having anything to eat tonight?"

Heather picked up her glass and went into the kitchen.

On the day of the wedding the nursing staff helped bathe and dress Iris. Heather and Jeff donned their outfits although Jeff had made do with the suit that he had worn at Claire and Sam's wedding no point in wasting money. The wheelchair was taken from the garage and dusted down. Iris was maneuvered down the stairs and plonked in to it with Jeff steering. The taxi arrived and the three set off to the registry office. There was a small group of friends of Claire's and Mikes brother from Scotland they all stood aside as Claire arrived in a white limousine with Charlie and Luke.

Claire wore a beige lacy dress; she had wanted to arrive with the children rather than her dad as tradition called for. She had had a big wedding with Sam but it didn't mean anything, Mike was everything

that Sam wasn't, kind dependable calm romantic, he
hated anything violent even on the television. She
thought some people would think Mike was boring but
he wasn't he was just right for her.

The ceremony was ten minutes at the most
Iris claimed people hadn't time to take their coats off.

"Wham bam thank you mam" said Jeff

He was ready for a drink although there
wouldn't be much of that with this crowd. The
reception was held at Bishop Horton Golf Club in the
Gary Player suite just large enough to swing a four
iron. The thirty people mulled around until a bell was
rung with Dirty Dancing played on the sound system.
Everyone was happy for the couple and that Claire had
at last found true happiness.

"What happened to her last husband" asked
Iris

"They were divorced mother" whispered Jeff

"I liked him he used to buy me Dairy Box,
why did she get divorced"

"Things just didn't turn out "Jeff tried to
distract his mother

"I'll get you a drink mum what are you
having?"

"Do the children still see him? "she asked

"No mum"

"That's not right they should see their father"

Jeff didn't want to explain again what had
happened to Sam

"What about a nice Sweet sherry?"

"What with my legs I don't think so I'll have a
brandy with a dry ginger, where is Heather I need her
for the toilet"

Jeff spoke to Heather then went to the bar
and ordered the drinks a brandy for his mother a
whiskey for himself and a tonic for Heather.

"Seventeen pounds eighty pence sir" the barman announced

"Bloody hell" Jeff pulled out a twenty pound note and reluctantly paid the barman. He was still grumbling when Heather returned with his mother

"I don't think we should stay long, mum needs her own space.

"It's our daughter's wedding Jeff, we have to stay"

The meal was served and enjoyed by the party. Iris could not eat the beef because it was too rare.

"It's got blood coming out of it they haven't cooked it Jeff "complained Iris

"It's supposed to be like that mum"

"No its not that's some trumped up sissy chef like Gordon Oliver's idea or them foreigner's idea not for good British beef"

After the meal had finished Jeff took Heather to one side

"Heather mother needs to go she's had enough"

Heather was furious

"I want to watch them have their first dance Jeff your mum does too"

Jeff sulked and went to the bar to drown his sorrows. It was an hour later that the DJ announced the bride and groom would take their first dance.

'Everything I do I for you' Bryan Adams voice rang out as the newlyweds danced an awkward robot type dance Heather had a tear in her eye. She thought they looked happy, Claire looking up to a very red faced Mike. Heather wasn't sure about Mike she hoped Claire would be happy and that the children had a good father at last. That is all any mother would want, that their children were happy, they didn't have to be successful just happy. Tom closed in on his mother

"She will be alright mum" he put his arm around her.

"I'm sure she will be, are you?" she looked into her sons eyes he smiled back

"Yes I'm great, sorry I haven't been around much I have spoken to Gran she seems ok, how are you coping?"

Heather raised her eye brows

"Its difficult Tom please come to see her now and again she must be bored to death laid in that bed day in and day out.

"I will mum but you know it is with the business you have to be on top of it constantly.

"I know Tom" Heather was disappointed with her son as soon as he had been married it was as though he had divorced his family.

"Come on mum are we ready to go?" said Heather Iris had been parked in the corner with another Brandy.

The children arrived with bags and baggage the following day. Claire and Mike left for their honeymoon hand in hand. Heather would have to sleep in the same bed as Jeff for two weeks that was going to be a trial in itself. Snoring with the added torment of cigarette fumes and a whiskey vapour.

Luke had the put you up bed while Charlie claimed the double bed.

"It's not fair "grumbled Luke

"Oh come on its only for two weeks" said Heather

She was surprised the children were as good as gold. They went to school with no problems did their homework when told and spent many hours with Iris who told them stories about when she was a girl.

Heather was able to catch up with her research on poisons drug effects and famous women criminals.

The two weeks passed very quickly Claire and Mike arrived home brimming over with happiness. They had brought Jeff a bottle of Whiskey from duty free, an embroidered cushion cover for Gran and a shell necklace for herself. The children were given new watches to screams and excitement.

Claire, Mike and the children left after enjoying one of Heathers roast dinners. Heather took a deep breath and shouted to Jeff in the lounge.

"I'm going into the bath" Jeff didn't answer. She went upstairs and ran the bath adding a huge blob of bubble bath that smelt of vanilla.

"Mmm wonderful "she said out loud as she undressed then dipped her toe into the steaming water. She breathed slowly the water caressed her body and she closed her eyes. Heather was content at that moment, Iris had enjoyed having the children around it was so much easier for her if someone else took some of the burden. Her peace was interrupted by a deafening banging on the door. Heather jumped out of the bath in one swift movement. Jeff's face was the colour of burnt ash.

"Heather quick Heather" she wrapped a towel around herself as she dripped suds onto the tiled floor.

"It's mum its mum "Jeff shouted "I just came up and put my head around the door"

Heather pushed past him into the bedroom, Iris laid with her mouth open gurgling

"What's wrong with her "shouted Jeff

"I think she is having another stroke Jeff ring the ambulance quick" Jeff jumped down the stairs to use the telephone while Heather held the hand of Iris.

"Jeff's called the doctor mum hold on, hold on"

161

A few minutes passed then Heather heard the ambulance siren, Jeff let them in by the front door.

"Hello Mrs Foster, Iris you are in good hands "said the ambulance man. With a monitor on her arm and chest Iris was transported to the hospital, Jeff accompanied his mother in the ambulance as Heather dressed and followed in a taxi. She had rung Tom and Claire to let them know what had happened to their grandmother.

Jeff and Heather sat in the corridor as doctors tended Iris. Heather couldn't believe her luck she would have to take another day off work tomorrow no doubt. Doctors met with the couple about an hour after Iris had been admitted.

"Mr and Mrs Foster your mother has suffered another stroke she is very ill, we will be admitting her there is not much you can do at the moment so I would suggest you go home and get some sleep and ring ward five tomorrow to find out about your mothers progress"

"Thank you Doctor" they said in uniformity.

"Bloody hell "said Jeff when they got home "our lives seem to go from one death to another"

"She isn't dead yet Jeff" said Heather

"She might as well be, what is she going to be like after this, her brain will have shut down"

He poured a large Whiskey.

"I'm not putting her in a home though. She belongs here with her loved ones; we will look after her"

We, thought Heather that's a good one.

"She will have to have full nursing care Jeff; I have to go to work how can we afford it?"

"We will, the kids will have to help out its their grandmother as well.

"They have enough on their plates, they have jobs, children, businesses"

"Stop molly coddling them Heather, we are a family that means everyone helps out" apart from you thought Heather.

Heather lay on the bed in the back bedroom Jeff had opened another bottle of Whiskey and she was sure he would finish most of it. Why was it always down to her to clear things up and manage it all? She thought it would be better if Iris died during the night she hoped she would, if not the burden of caring for yet another person would drive her insane.

The following morning Jeff had rung the hospital Iris was awake but was not responding very well to nurses. Heather had rung into work telling them that she would take a day's leave and why it was at such short notice. Nikki Farmer was very sympathetic and told her she could have the time as compassionate leave. Crikey thought Heather compassion that's a new word for her.

Tom picked both of them up to take them to the hospital he was visibly upset about his Gran, Heather thought it was touching. On reaching ward five the sister took them to Iris.

"Iris Iris your son is here"

Heather wondered who had given the nurse permission to call her mother in law by her first name instead of Mrs Foster, no one had any respect for the elderly these days. Iris opened her eyes and mouthed hello but no sound came out.

"Gran Gran its Tom" Tom took his grandmothers hand and kissed it. They spoke to the doctor who said it was early days, this was her second stroke so she was lucky to be alive.

Heather returned to work the following day and continued juggling hospital visits, cooking cleaning and babysitting. Jeff found it too difficult to go to the hospital it upset him too much so Heather went straight from work. Iris started to respond to treatment she was still unable to walk as before and now her right arm was paralyzed her speech had not returned so the hospital had assigned a speech therapist and a physio to help her with her recovery.

Iris had been in the hospital for three weeks when the doctors asked Jeff and Heather to attend a meeting on Iris's progress.

"Well Mr Foster have you thought about what will happen when your mother is well enough to be discharged" The doctor stared at Jeff waiting for a miracle answer.

"Well she will be coming home to us wont she Heather" Jeff turned towards Heather.

"What does the doctor say Jeff" she looked at the doctor silently begging him to say Iris wouldn't be able to return home. The doctor looked at Heather then at Jeff.

"She needs 24hr care so she would benefit from a nursing home they have the facilities"

Heather sighed noticeably, Jeff jumped up, "No my mother is not going into a home we will look after her, we will get care in, tell him Heather, my mother needs to be at home with her family around her."

"It will be very difficult Jeff as the doctor said we haven't the facilities"

"Well we will get them, you can hire hoists and things like that can't you doctor?"

The doctor nodded

"Well that settles it "Jeff sat down satisfied he had got his way. Heather would be able to do things in a morning before work and when she got home she was good at that. He could sit with his mother during the day and care staff could do the bathing, dressing, physio. He could see that Heather wasn't happy but it was his mother and as head of the household his word was law.

Heather felt as though her world had imploded yet again. She didn't want to argue in front of the doctor she would save it for later. The doctor said Iris could be discharged the following week in that time they arranged for care staff to be organized and equipment to be delivered. They arrived home in silence, Jeff was waiting for Heather to start the argument. Heather made a cup of tea for them both, Jeff poured himself a large Whiskey.

"Did you think it would be have been better to discuss the situation before you went head first into making a decision. "said Heather through her clenched teeth she was furious

"Heather it's my mother and I'm not putting her into a home, the whole family can help"

"And you think that is going to happen?"

"Do you know I didn't realise up until now how bloody selfish you are "he slurped his glass of Whiskey.

Heather stood with her mouth open, selfish she had spent most of her life looking after other people. She didn't give him the satisfaction of a full scale argument. She picked up her lap top and went to bed, he could get his own meal.

The next week went very , quickly. A commode and a hoist were delivered, a table on wheels and a seat for the bath. Heather was quiet at work at the prospect of even more work made her head ache. She ran her hand across the crime and murder section sign and thought of Jeff.

Heather had booked a day's leave for the day Iris was to be discharged, the ambulance men carried Iris up the stairs to the master bedroom.

"Hello mum its lovely to see you, you are home at last" chirped Jeff

"Hello mum" said Heather as she watched the frail body of her mother in law was lowered into the double bed.

"Hel, hel" Iris couldn't quite manage a full hello.

"I'll put the kettle on mum do you want a biscuit?"

"Cre, Cre" said Iris

"Cream Ones yes we have creamed ones" smiled Heather, poor bugger thought Heather.

Jeff sat by his mother's bed for almost half an hour, that must be a record thought Heather as she served the tea maybe he will do his duty after all.

After tea Tom and Sarah came to see their Gran then Claire, Mike and the children. Heather was busy in the kitchen making coffees when Claire popped her head around the door.

"Hi mum Gran seems happy she's home I must say you have taken something on there, will you be able to manage?"

"I will have too Claire, your dad wanted her to be here"

"But dads not looking after her"

"I know but I'll try my best" Claire threw her arms around Heather and gave her a hug, things were looking up.

CHAPTER
TWENTY FIVE

.
.

After a month Heather was exhausted she seemed to be in a constant daze. Jeff had managed to take the odd cup of tea up to his mother but found it difficult holding the beaker to her mouth. He was no good with illness he said over and over again. Heather was now rushing home at lunchtime and giving Iris soup or sandwiches as she couldn't trust Jeff to do it. Iris's health was not improving; physio came once a week but the feeling in her arm had not returned. Heather thought it would have been better that Iris had died from the last stroke it would have been kinder even animals were put down when they were in pain.

"I'm going in the bath Jeff" her husband didn't turn around just gave a grunt.

She bathed quickly and dressed in fresh pyjamas then wrapping herself in a fluffy dressing gown

She went into the master bedroom Iris lay rigidly in the bed Emmerdale was on the TV. Heather sat at the side of the bed.

"How are you mum?" she took the old woman's hand, she always found it awkward calling Iris mum but that it seemed disrespectful to call her Iris.

"We, we "stuttered Iris

"What's that mum, what do you want?"

"Hel, hel" strained Iris's voice

"Help" she managed to get the word out.

"Help you, yes what do you need help with?"

"Do you need a drink, something to eat?"

Iris shook her head she was determined to get Heather to understand. She shook her head she was determined to get Heather to understand. With her left hand she reached the table at the side of the bed Heather went around the bed and lifted things up in turn, tissues no, cup no, brush no, pills yes."

"You have had your pills for today mum"

"Help Hel" she stuttered again.

The doorbell rang it was the night care team. Heather went downstairs and made hot chocolate she was troubled by what had just happened. What did Iris want but she needn't ask the question to herself she knew what Iris wanted.

The two nurses made Iris comfortable

"She is a bit agitated tonight" said the plump nurse whose uniform bulged at the buttons. Ring the office if you need us to come back we are local tonight."

"I have given her an injection of morphine to settle her."

"I will" said Heather and closed the door behind them.

She stood at the foot of the stairs her hand on the newel post looking up to the door of the master bedroom. She then sat quietly at the dressing table in the back bedroom her cup of hot chocolate had a skin on the top of it. she brushed her hair slowly. She placed the brush back on the dressing table stood up and tightened her dressing gown cord around her waist.

As she turned the handle of the bedroom door there was a slight creak to the floorboards. Heather crept across the landing. In her hand the syringe of morphine left a red mark in her palm. Downstairs she could hear the television. She opened the door to the master bedroom. Iris slowly turned her head towards her.

"Medication time mum" Heather whispered, Iris looked at the clock she looked back at Heather.

Heather stood at the bottom of the bed and lifted the duvet she held Iris's foot and with one jab stuck the needle into the skin between the old woman's toes.

"I'm sorry Iris you are too much hard work, I'm tired your son couldn't do it either" Iris saw a slight smile on Heathers lips showing her teeth and making a grotesque face.

Heather stood at the foot of the bed breathing slowly and deeply as the old woman slipped away.

It was seven o'clock when Heather got up she showered and dressed then made tea for herself Iris and Jeff.

"Morning Mum" Heather cheerfully said as she pulled the velour curtains back. The sunshine streamed into the room and onto the body of her mother in law.

"She's dead isn't she Heather? Jeff was stood at the side of her.

"Yes" said Heather, "She's at peace."

Jeff knelt at the side of the bed and cried his weeping was interrupted by the front door bell.

"It's the nurses" said Heather

"They may be able to do something "cried Jeff

"No Jeff she is dead."

Heather let the two nurses in telling them they had just found Iris dead. The doctor was called and Heather made tea. Another day off work thought Heather.

Doctor Rashid comforted Jeff and said it had been expected and really it was a blessing she wasn't in pain anymore.

Heather could write the script for comforters, She's at peace, no quality of life, blah, blah, blah.

Claire, Mike, Tom and Sarah rolled up mid-morning, the funeral directors had been already and Iris had been taken to the chapel of rest.

Heather made sandwiches for the family and took her place in the kitchen. She felt a great burden lift off her shoulders. She was free, free at last then looked at the pile of sandwiches. After a couple of hours Heather and Jeff were left in the house. Heather stood at the sink washing the pots. In her head she was decorating the master bedroom pale lilac she thought. She returned back to earth with a bump.

"Heather Heather" she dried her hands on the tea towel and opened the lounge door.

"You could die of thirst in this house" Jeff held his mug above his head not taking his eyes from the television and Alaskan railway.

Heathers anger started in her hands as she clenched her fists her eyes burnt into the back of the chair as she watched the mug jingle in Jeff's hand.

Denise was born in West Yorkshire. Working for the local council in a number of roles including housing management and social services. She now divides her time between England and the Charente France.

16135110R00104

Printed in Poland
by Amazon Fulfillment
Poland Sp. z o.o., Wrocław